Mama Stalks
the Past

NORA DeLOACH

BANTAM BOOKS

NEW YORK TORONTO LONDON

SYDNEY AUCKLAND

This edition contains the complete text
of the original hardcover edition.
NOT ONE WORD HAS BEEN OMITTED.

MAMA STALKS THE PAST

A Bantam Book

PUBLISHING HISTORY
Bantam hardcover edition / December 1997
Bantam mass market edition / October 1998

ISBN-13: 978-0-553-57721-1

ISBN-10: 0-553-57721-2

Published simultaneously in the United States and Canada

Bantam Books are published by Bantam Books, a division
of Bantam Doubleday Dell Publishing Group, Inc. Its trade-
mark, consisting of the words "Bantam Books" and the
portrayal of a rooster, is Registered in U.S. Patent and Trade-
mark Office and in other countries. Marca Registrada. Bantam Books, 1540 Broadway, New York, New York 10036.

PRINTED IN THE UNITED STATES OF AMERICA

OPM   10 9 8 7 6 5 4 3 2

In Dedication:

To my wonderful family, who lovingly support me!

Thanks to my editor Kate Miciak, the master of all editors, whose help was invaluable. I could never have presented *Mama* as the sophisticated lady she is without Kate. Thanks to Amanda Clay Powers, Kate's Editorial Assistant, whose charm and assistance made it an easier task, and special thanks to my agent Denise Stinson, who aided in Mama's debut.

CHAPTER
ONE

I was pissed.

The temperature was thirty-eight, the wind-chill eighteen; gusts snatched my breath from my throat. With my gloved right hand I pumped gas; my left I tucked inside my coat to warm my tingling fingers.

Five minutes later I was crossing Wesley Chapel, my eyes following a plane that kissed the only thing on the November horizon, a thin cloud that looked like it had been sketched across the sky. A blast of frigid air through my Honda's window told me that I'd crossed the Interstate and pulled into the McDonald's drive-through. I took a deep breath before ordering black coffee.

A few minutes later, I was making a sharp right onto Interstate 20. I slipped in an Anita Baker CD, got caught up in her mood, and watched gold, brown, and rust leaves dance across the highway.

Let me introduce myself—My name is Simone Covington. I live in Atlanta and work as a paralegal. My boss, Sidney Jacoby, is a defense lawyer who dresses impeccably and whose entire domain is in absolute order except for one thing: Dandruff falls from his hair like soft new snow. Everybody who knows him feels obliged to flick the stuff from his very expensive jackets.

My reason for not being tucked under my new downy comforter this gray November day was that I was driving to Otis, South Carolina, to visit my parents. For two months I had been working sixteen-hour days on the legal defense of a young man Sidney was representing, the son of an Atlanta minister. Sidney had finally pulled together a case that he felt good about, so I asked him for three extra days to be added to my weekend.

He'd agreed. So I called Cliff, the guy I've been dating for the past few years. Cliff is a divorce lawyer who is working hard to become a partner in his firm. I don't know if that has anything to do with it, but he always ends up with the client who wants her lawyer to fly all over the United States whenever she suspects she's getting the short end of the detachment stick.

Anyway, when I told Cliff about my extra long weekend, he was elated. He, like me, was beginning to think that we might be losing what we had. Five days alone together was exactly what we needed.

Less than an hour later, however, things had soured. Cliff was flying to New York. His client, Mrs. Zwig, insisted that he come; she wanted to renegotiate a clause because she'd learned that Mr. Zwig's live-in secretary was pregnant: Mrs. Zwig was determined to use the baby as leverage.

Tired, disappointed, and as I said earlier, pissed, I was in the middle of trying to figure out what to do with my five days off when Mama called.

My Mama, whose name is Grace but who is called Candi by everyone because of a golden-brown complexion the color of candied sweet potato, promptly said, "Come home!"

"For what?"

"Rest," she said.

I took a deep breath. "I'd planned to do something more exciting with my time, thank you," I replied.

Mama's laugh had a mock to it. "Without Cliff, the most exciting thing you can do, Simone, is to rest!"

I took another deep breath. "Don't rub it in," I muttered, thinking of the things I'd planned for me and Cliff to do.

Mama's tone moderated as if she understood my frustration. "Really, Simone, your father and I haven't seen you in over two months."

She was right. My work with Sidney had not only cut into the time I would have spent with Cliff but my trips to visit my parents as well. "And you're dying to see me this weekend, right?" I said, still not willing to view visiting Mama and Daddy as a substitute for being with Cliff.

"James did say that he'd like to see you, yes."

Mama's voice was nondefensive. I had to concede that the only other thing I could think of to do with my five glorious days of freedom was to go to Lenox Mall. Sidney pays me a very good salary but whenever I'm depressed or harried, I spend money like the government, more than I earn. What served as a deterrent to me now was the slip from NationsBank on my desk. It was a twenty-six-dollar overdraft charge, which meant that even though I'd had trouble seeing Cliff and my parents during the past two months, I hadn't failed to find the time to spend a lot of money.

Mama was right, it would be wiser for me to come home to Otis than to go to Lenox Mall—at least not until my next payday.

When I arrived in Otis and walked into Mama's kitchen, I knew instantly that I'd made the right decision. Mama had done her thing. . . . The enticing scent of sweet potatoes, cinnamon, nutmeg, eggs, vanilla, and sugar blended enticingly with the hard, cold afternoon air. I would be easing a blade through a newly-baked pie in less than thirty minutes.

No sooner than I'd hugged Mama and taken off my coat, there were short anxious rings on the doorbell. Mama, who was filling the coffee-pot with filtered water, looked at me. I could tell from her expression she knew I wasn't in the mood for company. The next ring was a long sharp siren. Some moron was leaning on the bell. I bolted into the foyer and snatched open the door. Nat Mixon and a woman stormed past me and headed into Mama's kitchen. When I caught up with them, Nat was squared off in front of Mama, his raisin-colored finger pointing in her astonished face. "You're a wicked woman, Miss Candi! A *wicked* woman who took advantage of my Mama!"

Nat stood six feet tall with broad shoulders.

His wide nose was pierced; a tiny ruby sat on his nostril like a semiprecious booger. His short hair sprouted like uncut grass. He was dressed in a pair of jeans and a tan sweater jacket that had holes in each elbow. He had a thin scar, the result of a fight in which he took a nasty cut from a switchblade; it ran from his left cheek to the base of his neck. His smell was a mixture of old sweat and cheap cologne.

The woman with him wore what looked like a dark brown wool dashiki over a pair of slacks. Her hair was finger-sized shoulder-length cornrow braids. She stood behind Nat rubbing her arm, her eyes glued to Mama's face.

Mama lost her look of surprise. "Don't you talk to me like that, Nat Mixon," she snapped. "And take your dirty finger out of my face!"

Nat's hands waved. He breathed heavily and a muscle twitched beneath the scar on his cheek. "Sugarcoated words ain't for the likes of you, Miss Candi! You ain't no good. And I'm gonna tell the whole town what kind of woman you *really* are!"

"Nat Mixon," Mama retorted, "I know you're troubled, your mother dying and all, but there's no call for you to spread lies about me!"

Nat glared. "You ain't gonna get away with what you've done!"

Mama looked as if she couldn't believe what

she was hearing, especially in the sanctuary of her own kitchen. "Boy, what *are* you talking about?"

"You're nothing but a good-for-nothing *thief*!"

I feared Mama was going to burst. "Get out of my house!" she hollered.

Tears welled up in Nat's marble eyes. His fist clenched. This time when he spoke, his voice trembled. "You're gonna pay, Miss Candi, sure as you were born to die, you're gonna *pay* for taking what my Mama had!" A curtain was being dragged from the window of Nat's eyes, giving a glimpse into the depths of his bitter disappointment. Nat had been his mother's only child; his father had been killed. Hannah Mixon had raised her son to be self-indulgent. Now, thirty and unmarried, he was irresponsible and known for stumbling in and out of fights, most of which he lost, and now he was losing his fight with Mama.

Mama's voice tempered. "I never spoke a word to your mother!" she told Nat, more gently.

Veins throbbed at Nat's temples. His nostrils flared. There was a crazed look on his face, one that made me decide I'd better do something fast. I took a gulp of air and cleared my throat. "Nat," I said, pulling out a can of roach spray from the kitchen cabinet, "you'd better get out of here!" I positioned the can toward his eyes. If he tried to hit Mama, I'd spray them . . . a trick I'd learned in a rape defense class in Atlanta.

Nat's finger was shaking in Mama's face again. If he feared the roach spray, nothing in his threat revealed it. "My Mama wasn't smart enough to make a will without somebody like you showing her how to do it! You're gonna be sorry for what you did!"

My finger rested on the spray button. If he came one step closer . . .

But Mama was unafraid, unshaken. "Get out of my house this minute, Nat Mixon!" she said.

"You talked Mama into giving you everything—"

Mama's eyes blazed. "You're accusing me of something that I don't know *anything* about!"

"Give me back what's *mine!*"

At that moment, Daddy walked into the room and I began breathing lighter. "What's going on in here?" he asked, looking at Nat. "You're talking so loud they can hear you clear across town!"

Veins were popping through Nat's neck like ridges. "You ain't right, Miss Candi!" he declared hotly.

"Soon as I can make some sense of what Hannah's done, I'll give back whatever you think belongs to you!" Mama shot back.

"You've got everybody in this town fooled, thinking you're so much!"

Daddy, who had swiftly assessed the situation, now planted himself firmly between Nat and Mama. Mama glanced at Daddy but kept talking to Nat. "I don't want *anything* that Hannah left!"

"I'm gonna kill you!" Nat yelled.

That was too much for my father. He moved closer to Nat and his hands balled into fists. "Don't you threaten Candi!" he roared at Nat.

Mama looked puzzled now. I think she couldn't believe what was happening. My hand tightened on the roach spray.

Nat took one step backward. His eyes sent a terrible message: I knew he could shoot Mama and watch her kick without feeling any remorse. "All I've got to say is that you'd better sleep with one eye open!" he snarled.

Daddy's body tensed to take a swing at Nat. I swallowed the lump in my throat. We were seconds from Daddy and Nat throwing down in a fistfight and we all knew it. Fortunately, Nat seemed bewildered by this sudden turn of events. I suspected something in his past experience warned him against hooking up with my father. Anyway, he took a loud ragged breath, then turned to face the woman who'd come in with him. She seemed to understand and shook her head. Without another word or threat, Nat turned and followed her into the foyer and out the front door.

After they'd gone, Mama sighed. "Nat's been drinking since Hannah died," she told Daddy and me.

I put the roach spray back into the cabinet, examined my hands to make sure that none of the poison had gotten on them. Not satisfied, I went to the sink to wash them. Wiping my hands dry, I glanced out the window. Afternoon shadows had begun to settle. I studied the house next door, a house that for the past five years had been occupied by the recently deceased Hannah Mixon and her son Nat. Lights burned in the living room; every other room was dark.

"He smelled like a distillery," I said, wondering about Nat's female companion. What part did she play in his outburst?

Daddy, who had followed Nat and the woman to the front door and set the security alarm, scowled. "If he keeps plucking my nerves, I'll beat that boy's behind until it's sober!"

I turned from the window. "Mama, you'd better tell the sheriff about Nat's threat. Just in case he tries something."

"Candi doesn't need Abe," Daddy snapped. "Nat ain't crazy enough to try to hurt her!"

I wasn't so sure about that. Nat Mixon and I

weren't friends, but I'd had several chats with him on previous visits home. He was impulsive, especially when he was drinking—I didn't trust him or his judgment in the least. "What *will* was he talking about?" I asked.

Mama answered me. "I got a phone call from the lawyer Calvin Stokes this afternoon. Stokes told me that Hannah made a will and—"

"I didn't know that Miss Hannah was smart enough to make a will," I interrupted.

Mama shook her head at my comment. "Other than Nat, *I am the only person Hannah named in her will!*"

I threw my head back and laughed. "Nat thinks you talked his mother into leaving you everything she owned?"

Mama looked annoyed and her tone cut my laugh short. "The whole thing is stupid—I mean, I didn't even *know* Hannah Mixon. Why would she put me in her will?"

"The way Nat's carrying on, maybe she left you something valuable," I said.

Mama wasn't impressed. "Why would Hannah Mixon leave me *anything* at all?" she argued, then walked over to the oven and pulled out a pair of sweet potato pies.

Daddy walked out of the room, I suspected to the hall bathroom.

The aroma of Bavarian chocolate coffee

quickly mingled with the mouth-watering smell of the pies. After she put them on the counter to cool, Mama poured herself a cup of freshly brewed coffee. "Hannah lived like a hermit! I never once was invited into her home."

I joined Mama at the coffeepot. "I can't believe you, the Good Samaritan of Otis, never visited your next-door neighbor."

"Once I tried to take her a bowl of my home-made soup. That woman looked out of her window right into my face and didn't answer her door!"

I decided not to wait for the pies to cool. I love hot sweet potato pie. "You're exaggerating!"

"*I am not!*"

I opened my hands in submission. Mama clearly wasn't in the mood for playful disagreement. "Then the good Miss Hannah was touched in the head. Nobody sane refuses your soup, Mama."

"I tried to be friendly," Mama insisted. "I really did!"

"You might have misunderstood—"

"SIMONE," Mama said hotly, "HANNAH MIXON HATED ME!"

Daddy walked back into the kitchen and I cut a generous piece of the pie for each of us. He set a cup of coffee down on the table and pulled out a chair. "Candi, I wouldn't take that too personal if I was you. Talk is that there weren't many people Hannah liked. And fewer that liked her!"

Mama shook her head, troubled. "I hope Calvin Stokes can shed light on what Hannah had on her mind. I couldn't stand the thought of people thinking I'd taken advantage of an old woman!"

I sat at the table next to Daddy, took a bite of my pie, and sipped from my coffee. The rich taste slid over my tongue. "Just get Calvin to give Nat whatever his mother left to you," I told Mama.

Her head tilted. "That can't be much. That old house, a few pieces of furniture!"

Daddy scowled like he was remembering his encounter with Nat. "Whatever it is Hannah left you, Candi, sign it right over to that fool Nat before I have to jack him up!"

Mama folded her arms across her breasts. "Calvin wants to see us first thing Monday morning, James. You can be sure that I'll give Nat back whatever Hannah left me. And that will be the end of all this nonsense from him!"

Daddy's scowl deepened.

"You look like you just sucked a lemon," I told him.

He fiddled with the handle of his coffee mug.

"I was just wondering who that woman with Nat was."

"I was going to ask you or Mama the same thing."

"Candi?" Daddy asked, looking toward Mama.

Mama shook her head. "My guess is she's some kin to Nat."

Daddy shrugged. "Hannah was a strange bird. Talk is that Abe ordered an autopsy on her body."

Mama's eyebrow rose. Abe Stanley was the Otis County sheriff. "You think Abe suspects something suspicious about Hannah's death?" she asked. Her tone reminded me of the relationship she had developed with the sheriff shortly after she and my father had settled in town.

The day was hot, she had said, the heat desert-like. Patches of gnats darted along the highway. Mama had just driven onto the Cooswhatchie River bridge, where trees hang on both sides and form a thick green cascade. She was noticing how the sunlight streamed through their branches, casting dancing shadows, when she heard a bang followed by the sound of flapping—her front tire had blown. She pulled her car to the shoulder jus. as Sheriff Abe and his deputy, Rick Martin, drove by. They stopped and the sheriff made Rick change Mama's tire. Grateful, Mama baked them a sweet potato pie that afternoon and delivered it to the sheriff's office. They loved it. Mama baked another. Soon her pies and their delivery became a weekly ritual. During her visits, the sheriff happened to mention a couple of unsolved petty crimes. After a few suggestions from Mama, the good sheriff figured out who was behind them. Sheriff Abe learned to respect Mama's opinion, which she has always called her sleuthing intuition. Now, whenever something comes up that the sheriff can't figure out, he asks Mama's opinion. She loves it.

If Daddy was remembering Mama's little hobby of crime solving, he didn't show it. Instead, he rolled his shoulders like they were stiff, maybe aching. "You can't believe everything you hear at Joe's barbershop," he said, as if an afterthought. "Hannah probably died of a heart attack like Dr. Clark said she did."

The phone rang. Mama crossed the room and answered it. Daddy put the last bite of pie in his mouth and stood to put on his jacket. Mama held up her hand, gesturing to him not to leave. After a moment, she hung the phone on its receiver, then wiped her forehead.

I pushed my empty coffee cup away.

Mama's eyes were wide, clear, the blacks and

whites pure, separate. My heart skipped. I knew that look—Mama's sleuthing intuition had been stirred. "That was Abe," she told us, her voice low. "He just got the results of Hannah's autopsy—she didn't die of a heart attack. Somebody pumped her full of poison!"

CHAPTER
TWO

I moved my head and cracked an eye. Darkness blanketed the room. I sat up, yawned, and looked at the clock. Two A.M. I heard the noise, the same one that had just shaken me from my deep sleep. I was not in Atlanta. I was in Otis.

The aroma of hazelnut coffee tingled my nostrils. I slipped out of bed. Mama sat at her kitchen table, her hand cupped around a mug.

I touched her shoulder. "Can't sleep?" I asked.

Mama looked up. "No."

I yawned again, stretched, then made a beeline to the cabinet where she kept her dishes and got a mug. "Any more pie?" I asked hopefully.

Mama pointed to a Tupperware cake plate on

the ceramic-tiled counter. Then she took off her glasses and rubbed her eyes the way she always does when she's trying to figure out something. Her brow was furrowed.

"What's on your mind?" I asked her.

"Hannah Mixon!"

"You may be a rich woman," I teased. "Hannah might have left you a fortune!"

Mama stroked the side of her cheek with her fingertips, then raised one eyebrow in a slant that was clearly a signal that she was not in a joking mood. "Why would that woman leave me anything?"

"You were neighbors," I pointed out.

"I told you, I didn't even know that woman!"

I didn't say anything, I headed for the coffee and pie. When I'd gotten my treats and was sitting at the table next to Mama, I reached over and touched her arm. "Mama, Miss Hannah must have thought a lot of you to leave you in her will," I said, trying to sound sanctimonious instead of funny.

"Hannah Mixon wasn't that kind of a woman!"

"Okay, then she was crazy, but who cares, she remembered you in her will!"

Mama spoke as if she was thinking out loud. "I don't like it," she mused. "Something in the milk ain't clean."

"Two can play the cliché game," I retorted cheerfully. "Don't look a gift horse in the mouth."

"Hannah Mixon ain't never given anybody except Nat anything," Mama said sourly.

"She might have had a change of heart."

"She was pure selfishness."

"That's a bit strong, don't you think?"

"Simone, trust me, Hannah Mixon had something up her sleeve." She dropped her glasses back on the bridge of her nose and fiddled with them until they were comfortable. "The thing that bothers me is that people might believe I influenced her—you know, talked her into giving me her things!"

Mama's tone made me realize that I'd misjudged her feelings about Daddy's decision to move back to Otis. I remembered the day eight years earlier when I had stumbled in on their conversation. My father had been stationed at Beal Air Force Base in California. He was saying, "Our boys Will and Rodney are doing okay, and Simone is almost finished high school. Thirty years is enough to give Uncle Sam's Air Force, Candi. I've decided to retire."

"Fine," Mama had told him. "But we've got to think of Simone."

"What about Simone?" Daddy asked.

"I was hoping we could settle where Simone plans to go to college."

"No," Daddy said. "I want to go *home*."

"Simone has already been accepted at Emory in Atlanta," Mama continued. "It's only a four-hour drive from Atlanta to Otis. You can visit home as often as you want."

"Otis is where we belong, Candi," Daddy insisted.

"We've lived in cities for so long . . . I don't know if I can adjust to going back to Otis, James. There's no more than five thousand people living within the town's limit."

"Five thousand *good* people," Daddy had pointed out.

Mama hadn't replied.

"Candi," Daddy argued, "I know you're worried about being away from Simone, but trust me on this one, she'll be all right. Like you said, we've lived in a lot of places, most of them crowded cities. Now that I'm ready to settle, I want to go home."

Still, Mama didn't say anything.

"You said yourself, Otis is real close to Atlanta. Go with me on this one, Baby, we ain't going to get too far from Simone." He paused. "I promise you, I ain't going to let nothing happen to our little girl."

I remembered thinking that since Mama

wasn't going to be happy in Otis, Daddy wasn't doing the right thing to take her there. Now, however, the concern in her voice about the town's reaction to Hannah Mixon's murder and the legacy she'd left Mama made me change my mind. Mama loved being in Otis, back home.

"Don't pay any attention to Nat," I told her now. "He's just bitter and selfish. You've done so much for the people in this town since you've returned. Everybody knows you're not the kind of a woman who would rob a crazy old woman."

"Whining Nat will make it sound like I befriended his mother just so that I could talk her into giving me her money. Certain people in this town like to hear that kind of stuff, especially since I—"

"Mama," I cut in sternly. "You're the one who's overreacting, don't you think?"

"Simone, it's *important* what my neighbors think about me!"

I touched her hand. "Come on, pretty lady," I coaxed, noticing without envy how her smooth skin and soft features made her look more like my sister than my mother. "This is the first time something like this has happened."

"What about those two old women who accused me of stealing their food stamps?"

"If my memory serves me right, those two

women accused *everybody* of stealing from them."

Mama gave me a long, searching look. "I've always wondered whether a few people still believe . . ." she faltered.

"Uncle Ben's trial made it clear that Aunt Agnes was behind those stolen food stamps," I said firmly. "Anyway, you must not have been the only person who didn't like Miss Hannah, 'cause somebody killed her."

Mama sighed and shook her head sadly. "I suppose what really concerns me is that Abe didn't call me about the poison until after he got the autopsy report."

"So?"

"That's not like Abe. Maybe . . ."

"Daddy said that Hannah attracted enemies."

"You think Abe knew about Hannah's will?"

"Mama, Abe Stanley is your friend!"

Mama sipped her coffee, but she didn't say anything. I decided to change the subject. "You didn't ask me about Sidney," I said.

"What is your boss up to now?" she demanded.

"He's got a new client, one we've been spending most of our time with over the past months."

"So?"

"This case has a hint of dirt to it, like an ink spot on a white blouse."

"Go on," Mama said. I could see she was still thinking about who might have murdered Hannah Mixon.

"Our client is the son of an Atlanta minister."

"What's so unique about that?"

"He's been charged with killing a young Korean prostitute."

Mama's fingers drummed on the table. "And?"

"Sidney believes he's been set up."

"Why would anybody do that?" she asked.

"When we find the answer, we'll find the real killer," I said.

Mama looked funny, like the wheels in her head were spinning but whatever they were on to, it had nothing to do with Sidney or his client.

At ten o'clock Monday morning, my parents, Nat, and I were sitting in Calvin Stokes's law office, an office that's located over Casey Drug Store on Lee Street.

Calvin is a tall white man with a bearded face and blond hair over one of his eyes. His forehead is broad and unlined, his eyebrows light commas over his deep-set, very blue eyes. The only wrinkles on his face are barely noticeable crow's-feet.

Calvin is Otis County's rags-to-riches son. His father was a small-time soybean farmer;

young Calvin dreamed of becoming a lawyer. He graduated from Otis High School, then joined the Army. After he was discharged, he went to the University of South Carolina, then on to law school. Eight years later he came back home to stay, home to practice law.

Calvin's firm consists of himself. The bulk of the day-to-day work is taken care of by a legal secretary, Louise Barker. There is also a receptionist named Norma Jenkins, a graduate of Salkehatchie in Clairmont.

Everybody in Otis used Calvin for legal matters: Hannah Mixon had come to him to make her will.

Calvin's office is large, with plenty of windows, lots of clean white space, and a dark green carpet in an expensive wool. Framed watercolors decorate the walls.

Now Calvin appraised his desk, then moved the marble pen holder a half inch to the left. "Nat," he began, "I'm sorry I didn't get to this thing before now. I've been out of town for the past three weeks. I didn't hear about your poor mother's death until early Friday morning."

Nat scowled.

Calvin looked from Nat to Mama. "I called you both as soon as I could," he continued.

"When did Hannah make this will?" Mama asked him.

"Two months ago," Calvin replied.

"What made her do it?" I asked.

Calvin shook his head. "I asked Hannah the same thing. She, well, she . . ."

Nat fidgeted in his chair. He wouldn't look at Mama. "I ain't stupid. You and Miss Candi is thieving me together. *You* talked Mama into leaving everything to Miss Candi, didn't you?"

Calvin looked at him. When he spoke, his words were somber. "Hannah didn't leave *everything* to Grace," he said.

Nat's eyebrows went up and he sat forward in his chair, the surprise on his face shining.

"Let me read the will and you'll see what your Mama had in mind."

Calvin began:

"*I, Hannah Mixon, being of sound mind, leave my house, my furniture, my insurance policies, and whatever cash I have to my son, Nat Mixon.*"

Pleased, Nat grinned.

"*I leave two hundred and fifty acres to Candi Covington, my next-door neighbor. Candi Covington cannot sell or will this land to any other person for five years from the date of my death.* That's it," Calvin finished.

There was absolute silence in the law office. Then Nat roared: "She left Miss Candi the best part!"

Calvin gave us a helpless look as he brushed

his pale hair from his eye. He turned his palms up.

"M-my Mama wasn't crazy," Nat stuttered. "All of you are in this together, trying to steal my land!"

"Nat, please—" Mama began.

Nat wailed, "You're a thief and I'm going to tell the whole town what you are!"

That was too much for Mama. "Shut up and let me finish talking!" she snapped. "I've never had one conversation with your mother. How could I have *talked* her into *anything*?"

But Nat wasn't convinced. He started shaking his finger at Mama again. "You think I'm stupid!"

Mama's eyes widened. "Don't you point that—"

"You're not going to get away with this!" Nat yelled, jumping out of his chair and towering over Mama.

Daddy'd had enough. "NAT," he shouted, "SIT DOWN!"

Nat, who had swollen up like a bullfrog, looked into Daddy's glaring eyes. Then he sat down.

Calvin took a deep breath, glad that things seemed temporarily under control. He moved the marble pen holder another half inch to the left. "There it is," he said. "Oh, yeah, Abe called me Friday afternoon and—"

Mama shook her head, signaling Calvin not to mention what the sheriff had told him. I realized that her question to me on Friday night had been answered. Abe Stanley did know about the will and its strange provision before he had called Mama two days ago to tell her that Miss Hannah had been poisoned.

Daddy scratched his head. "This is crazy," he muttered.

"Nothing about this whole thing makes sense!" Mama said softly.

Nat was breathing heavily. He shot a look at Mama, one that made her reach over and touch his arm. "I don't know why your mother did what she did," she told him firmly, in the tone of voice you use when you talk to a bad-tempered child.

"Ain't nothing but you talked her into doing something against me," Nat insisted.

"I never spoke once to your mother."

"Yeah, right!" Nat said sourly.

"I'll prove that I don't want your land. I'll sign it over to you right now!" Mama turned to Calvin.

But Calvin shook his head. "Can't do that, Grace. Not for five years."

Nat growled deep in his throat.

There was a look of determination in Mama's eyes that I knew very well. "There must be a way to get around that stipulation," she said.

"I'll check into it," Calvin told her, "but Judge Thompson doesn't like breaking wills."

Nat's mouth formed a grudging line. "I've got obligations," he said bitterly.

"Use the insurance money you've got," Daddy snapped. "Sell the house if you have to."

"Nat," Mama said, sounding a little embarrassed. *"Please, don't tell people that Hannah left me that land!"*

Nat's eyes moved around the room. His breathing rasped. He shifted in his seat.

"If you tell anybody . . . *one soul* that Hannah left me those two hundred and fifty acres I won't give it back to you," Mama said, probably reading his mind. It wasn't hard to see that Nat Mixon intended to make trouble.

Nat's eyes narrowed. There was an ugly light in them.

"I'm not kidding," Mama continued. "If I hear a *whisper* from one person in this town that Hannah left me that land I'll call Calvin and tell him to stop trying to break the will . . . I mean it!"

Nat pouted.

"Boy, if you keep this thing quiet," Daddy said, "you'll get your land soon as Calvin talks the judge into breaking Hannah's five-year stipulation. I'll see to it personally."

Mama looked at Calvin.

"I'll start working on it today," Calvin promised, and I knew he would.

Nat stared at Mama, as if he'd never seen her before. Then he muttered reluctantly, "Okay, I won't tell nobody."

So, why didn't I believe him?

Daddy leaned back. "Then we understand each other, don't we?"

Nat got to his feet, rubbing his forehead with the heel of his hand, as though wiping away sweat. Today he had replaced his shabby clothes with a somewhat threadbare suit, but the ruby still gleamed in his nostril. "If that's all you got to tell me, can I go now?" he asked us all, nastily.

Calvin spoke. "You can do whatever you want with everything else Hannah left."

Nat glanced at Mama, nodded, then slammed out the door. Calvin cupped his chin in his hand. He sighed. "Now that he's gone, Grace, I have to say that Hannah was not herself when she made this will."

"What do you mean?" Mama asked.

Calvin frowned. "Let's just say I wasn't surprised when Abe told me she had been murdered."

We stared at him in astonished silence. What

29

on earth could he mean? From everything we'd heard and seen, Hannah Mixon had been a sour, unfriendly woman, but who would have wanted to kill her? Things like that just don't happen in Otis.

"There was something else," Calvin continued. "Hannah told me that she wanted you to look in the house for an envelope, Grace."

"An envelope?" Daddy asked. "What's in it?"

"Hannah wouldn't say," Calvin replied.

"Why didn't she just give it to you or to Abe?" Daddy asked.

"When Hannah came to my office that day and told me what was on her mind about the will, I tried to talk her out of it. But my reluctance just seemed to make her more determined. Maybe she didn't trust me with whatever's in that envelope. Or Abe, either. But whatever it is, it seemed very important to her that you look for it, Grace." He shook his head and sighed again.

"The whole thing is so secretive, just like something crabby old Hannah would concoct," Daddy said.

"Hannah had an edginess about her," Calvin agreed. Because Sidney has more than one crazy client, I knew Calvin's words hid a lot more than they betrayed.

"I don't know why we've got to get mixed up with this mess," Daddy objected. "Let Abe find who killed her. You just figure out a way for Candi to give Nat back his land so we'll be out of this thing."

Calvin sighed. "As I said, I'll talk to Judge Thompson about breaking the will, but frankly I can't promise you much of anything. The judge doesn't like making exceptions. Says once he starts there will be no end to how far he'll have to go to satisfy hungry relatives."

Mama spoke as if she were totally unaware of the conversation that had just taken place between my father and the lawyer. "There is one person in this town who's a killer. And it seems that spiteful Hannah has put me to work finding him!" she murmured.

CHAPTER
THREE

Mama is a case manager at the Otis County Department of Social Services. She worked toward a degree through the University of New York External Degree program, which allowed her to take her required courses at whatever accredited college she could attend as my father was transferred from Air Force base to Air Force base across the country. Seven years and as many universities later, she obtained her bachelor's degree with a major in sociology.

Although Mama loves helping people, I know that her real passion is digging up bits and pieces until she's solved a mystery, and there's nobody better at doing that. Long ago, I don't remember when, Mama decided that if we could get at the truth of a problem, we would have made a contribution to humankind. Most of the time I agree with Mama. This time, however, finding the truth about Hannah Mixon's murder almost cost Mama her life.

It was eleven o'clock when we left Calvin's office. We drove to the West End, filled my tank with gas, then stopped at Echerd's, where Mama picked up a couple of get-well cards and chatted with the girl at the cash register.

When we got back to the house, Daddy went straight into his room, Mama headed for her kitchen, and I curled up in my bedroom to call Cliff in New York. "How are things going?" I asked him. My voice sounded as dark as my mood.

"Not good," he answered. His voice had an edge to it, a tone I notice whenever he's under pressure.

I took a deep breath, then let it out slowly. "What's wrong?"

"Mrs. Zwig wants to throw out everything we've pulled together, start from scratch."

"Because of the baby?" I asked, meaning the baby Mr. Zwig had fathered with his just-out-of-high-school secretary.

Cliff cleared his throat. "That's what she says."

I began playing with the fringes on the handmade crocheted bedspread I had gotten Mama from Nassau when Cliff had talked me into making a wonderful impromptu trip several months earlier. "You sound doubtful."

"I don't know," he replied, his speech slow and deliberate. "I've got mixed feelings about a woman who talks about a child like it's a piece of property."

I sat up in the bed. "What's your next move?"

"I'm talking to Mr. Zwig this afternoon," he said.

"So, we won't get to spend *any* time together? Our whole five days go down the drain?"

"I'll let you know how things are shaping up, Simone. I'd like to be back in Atlanta tomorrow. Maybe we can spend Wednesday together. What do you think?"

"Don't ask me what's going on in my mind," I said. "Ask me how *bad* I want to see you!"

Half an hour later, I put the phone back on its receiver and joined Mama in the kitchen. Although the succulent aroma of stew and baked bread was delightful, food wouldn't take care of my need to be with Cliff.

Mama's kitchen is shaped like an *L*, the working space on the long side, the stove, oven, and grill on the short. Mama was standing over her pot, dipping a wooden spoon inside and drawing up a taste. I couldn't help but think how much magic seems to go into her cooking. I wondered why the gift hadn't been passed on to me.

"Where's Daddy?" I asked. Mama looked up, then walked over to the sink and turned on the hot water.

"He changed clothes, grabbed a sandwich, then left, as he said, to take care of business," she answered, dunking the long wooden spoon under the faucet.

"You nor I can keep up with our men today."

Mama laughed softly. "You know where Cliff is. And I know where James is heading."

"What good is it to know where they are when they're not here!"

Mama turned to face me. "When do you expect Cliff back in Atlanta?"

"He's going to try to come home tomorrow."

Mama's eyebrow raised. "Oh," she said.

"I'm going back to Atlanta first thing tomorrow morning." At least Cliff and I might have one day together, I thought, trying to shake my bad mood. "Is that stew ready?"

Mama smiled. "Get bowls while I get the bread from the oven."

We were almost five minutes into eating when I noticed Mama's attention had drifted away from the story I was telling her about how the police had caught the minister's son hiding out in his basement. "What are you thinking?" I asked.

"I was hoping that big-mouthed Nat keeps his promise. I'd hate to think of what Sarah Jenkins, Carrie Smalls, and Annie Mae Gregory will do with the news about Hannah's land."

I held my fork in midair and grinned. Despite Mama's using these three women whenever she needed information about other people in the area, she never liked that they knew everything about everybody. "You're not begrudging your sources, are you?" I teased.

"When those three get to talking, they don't care whether what they say is a lie or the truth!"

"You *listen* to them," I pointed out.

"Simone, I take what they say with a grain of salt, you know that!" Her tone was unexpectedly sharp.

"You talked with those ladies lately?" I asked.

"I ran into them at Winn Dixie on Friday afternoon before you got here," she said.

"What news did they bear?" I knew Mama would have made good use of her encounter with Otis's best source of local information. Sarah Jenkins, Carrie Smalls, and Annie Mae Gregory knew everything about everyone in Otis. Or pretended to.

"Annie Mae Gregory did mention that Hannah had been married four times."

I shoved my spoon into the stew. It was rich and dark, bubbling with meat and carrots, and new potatoes. "You know, you may not have to spend too much time on Miss Hannah, Nat, or that land," I told her. "Once you find the envelope Miss Hannah told Calvin Stokes about, things will straighten out, don't you think?"

"The solution to Hannah's murder won't be as simple as finding an envelope."

I sipped the wonderful broth. My mind drifted to Cliff and how much I wanted to be with him. Life was the pits, I thought.

Mama looked as if she understood my feelings, as if she knew exactly what was on my mind. She broke a piece of bread in two, then said, "I'll give Nat a day or two to calm down before I ask him to let me go through his mother's things."

I frowned. "Why?"

"He's so uptight."

I shook my head. "I know enough about Nat to know that he's not only impulsive but greedy. A few days will be too late."

Mama leaned back in her chair and smoothed her napkin on her lap. "You're right—he's probably combing through Hannah's belongings right now, looking for whatever he can turn into cash. And if he finds the envelope he won't understand what is inside."

"He could throw it away," I warned.

Mama fidgeted in her seat. An odd look crossed her features. "To be honest, I would rather look for the envelope when he's not at home," she admitted.

"I'll go along with that," I said, eyeing the succulent piece of meat positioned on my fork. Nobody made stew that tasted like Mama's.

"Maybe later tonight . . . around eight," Mama suggested. "Nat usually leaves about that time and doesn't come back until the next morning."

I froze, remembering Nat's vengeful attitude and the stab of anxiety I'd felt when he came into our house angry. "On second thought," I said, "it might be a good idea to have Daddy close by when you go over to Miss Hannah's."

Mama's laugh was rich. "Nat *is* scared of James, isn't he?"

"Like a dog of a dogcatcher."

Mama nodded. "If we'll have to wait until James is here to go with us, we'll have to look for that envelope later than eight o'clock."

"The business my father has to take care of will take him more than a few hours, won't it?"

Mama spoke softly but quick. "James is hanging with his drinking buddies again," she admitted. Worry tinged her voice.

I wiped my mouth with the napkin, and felt a little guilty that all I had been worrying about was my troubles with Cliff. "I suspected that," I admitted.

"I've got to come up with some way to break the cycle," Mama said softly.

The expression on her face tugged at my heart. I patted her hand. "You know, psychologists call a person like you a codependent," I told her gently.

"James is my husband!"

"I'm sorry," I said. "I know that. And I know that you can handle it."

"Yeah," Mama murmured, as if talking to herself. "But I wonder if there will ever be a time when James will be able to handle it himself!"

I was silent. My father's drinking wasn't a source of contention between him and Mama. Mama didn't argue, she didn't fuss. For a long time, whenever my father came home drunk, she did her best to make him comfortable. But after his drinking almost landed him in jail for murder, it became clear she had decided that it was her responsibility to keep him sober. She never admitted it, but I knew it was a burden, one she insisted on bearing alone.

"By the way," I said, after a few moments of silence during which we cleaned our plates, "how will we get inside Miss Hannah's house if Nat isn't home?"

Mama smiled; her eyes and face sparkled. She was once again herself, eager to push ahead. "Now, that's a good question."

"I ain't up for spending time in jail for breaking into his house."

"We won't break in," Mama said firmly.

"Now that I think of it, I don't know if I like the idea of going into the house where that old woman was poisoned," I said.

"The house is harmless, Simone. It's her killer you need to fear."

"Everybody is so neighborly in town. Somebody must have really hated Hannah Mixon to bump her off like that," I pointed out.

"There was always talk about the spiteful things Hannah did to people," Mama murmured.

"Like what?" I, like Mama, had never spoken to Hannah Mixon in the five years she'd lived next to my parents. But I well remember her pinched, narrow face and unripe-apple sour scowl.

"Well, she called the police on the children in the neighborhood. Mr. Brown swears she tried to poison his two German shepherds, and people caught her dumping trash in their yards. I know for a fact that Mr. Jeffers swore that if one more thing happened between him and Hannah Mixon, he was going to make it miserable for her to continue living around here." Mama shook her head.

"She sounds like she was a crab, but that's no reason for somebody to poison her."

"I'm not trying to justify her murder, Simone. I'm trying to say that her killer might have had a motive. One thing for sure, whoever killed Hannah had no emotion while doing it. Putting that arsenic in her food wasn't a crime of passion, it was cold and very cruel. Abe said that there were no signs of a struggle, so it could have been somebody Hannah perceived as a friend."

"Did she have any friends?"

"I don't think she had many visitors. Be honest, Simone, I knew very little about my neighbor," Mama said.

"You knew she stirred up the neighborhood."

"Yes, but there must have been more to Hannah Mixon. I suppose the best thing to do is to contact my sources—"

"Miss Sarah Jenkins, Annie Mae Gregory, and Carrie Smalls," I interrupted gleefully.

"I've got the feeling that Sarah, Annie Mae, and Carrie knew a great deal about Hannah Mixon," Mama said. "You know, Simone, something keeps surfacing in my mind. There is an old saying that if you want to know a person, examine his behavior. Hannah was mean to everybody else, but she did love Nat. It just doesn't make sense that she didn't leave him that property."

I walked to the refrigerator and pulled out the water pitcher.

"Do you realize its market value? If there's timber to be cut from that land, it could make a person very rich!" Mama continued.

"True." I poured a glass of water. "But what harm could Hannah have thought would come to Nat by owning it?"

Mama walked over to the window and straightened the curtain. "The selling price for prime farm and timberland around here is probably thousands of dollars."

"The words 'thousands of dollars' would blow Nat's mind."

"That boy owes everybody in town," Mama agreed. "I feel sorry for him. Hannah did Nat an injustice by never making him finish school or teaching him how to work. Now that she's gone, he doesn't know how to do anything for himself."

"He knows how to spend money," I retorted. "I bet that whatever money he'll get from the insurance will be gone in six months."

"Sooner," Mama murmured, turning to look back out the window. Then her body stiffened and she said urgently, "Come here!"

I joined her at the window. From across the street, a man walked casually, stepping toward the front door of the white-and-green Mixon house. But the man didn't ring the bell. Instead, he waited. Then, after a minute, he reached out, twisted the knob. The door opened. The man stood motionless. Then, without going inside, he closed the door, turned, and walked quickly away from the house, down Smalls Lane.

I touched Mama's arm. "Who was that?"

"Moody Hamilton," Mama answered.

"Who?"

"Moody's people are from around Pleasant Hill, near Darien. He was raised by his grand-mother, who died last fall."

"Is he like Nat?" I asked.

Mama shook her head, knowing instantly what I meant. "Moody is not known for trouble. As a matter of fact, people say he's got a soft heart, kind and gentle."

"What's he doing at Nat's house?"

"Looking for Nat, I guess."

I rolled my eyes. "I bet Nat owes him money and he's wanting to collect, poor feller."

Mama frowned. Her golden-brown complex-ion took on a darker hue. "I'm not worried about

Moody," she told me. "It's Nat that concerns me. . . . It's not smart for him to leave his front door open like that!"

"I kind of thought that Moody was going inside."

"I don't know why he didn't. Nat's home." Mama pointed. "See, he's in the kitchen near the stove." She shook her head, then picked up the phone and dialed. "Nat," she said, once it was answered. "This is Miss Candi. . . . Listen, I just saw Moody Hamilton at your door. . . . Well, it's a good idea to keep your front door locked. He started to walk right in. . . . You're right, I'm not your mother."

Mama replaced the receiver.

I burst out laughing. "I know you didn't expect thanks for that call, did you?"

Mama smiled. But the expression in her eyes remained thoughtful. "At least we know we won't have a problem *getting* into his house tonight."

For the next half hour, as Mama and I cleaned the kitchen, I found myself looking toward the Mixon house time and time again. When the telephone rang, I answered because I was nearest to it. "Okay," I said, putting my hand over the receiver and turning to Mama, who had just put the last cup into the dishwasher. "It's Daddy's cousin Agatha," I told her.

Mama took a deep breath, then reached for the receiver. "Agatha, how are you? . . . Uncle Chester? No, James isn't at home. Now? Okay, Simone and I will be right over."

"What's that all about?" I asked, when she'd hung up.

"Uncle Chester is having a hissy fit," Mama said. She looked annoyed.

"Why?"

"Josiah Covington, your great-grandfather, owned over a thousand acres of land. When he died, his will left that land jointly to his twelve children. These twelve children could either farm the land, cut the timber and share the money from it, or even build a house on it, but they couldn't sell it, according to Josiah's will. Your daddy's father, Samuel Covington, was the first of those twelve children to die. And Uncle Chester is the last of those twelve children living. Your father, Agatha, Gertrude, and Fred Covington are the next generation of over one hundred heirs of those twelve children who are now scattered all over the country. Cousin Agatha is worried."

I was trying to sort out the tangled Covington family tree. "Why?"

"She's scared that once Uncle Chester dies, the land will be cut up and sold. So she has talked to Calvin Stokes to find out the best way to keep that from happening. Calvin suggested that the Covington Land Company be formed and that it be incorporated, and a Trustee be appointed. The Trustee would take care of paying the taxes, cutting the timber, and—"

"Cousin Agatha might be jumping the gun," I said.

"A couple of months ago there was a big dispute over heirs' property in Stewart County. Things were so bad that sisters and brothers wouldn't even sit together at their mother's funeral. Cousin Agatha doesn't want that kind of thing tearing our family apart when Uncle Chester dies. She doesn't want the land sold or lost for taxes either."

"The Covington family would never fight over property," I declared.

Mama's lips pursed. "Don't be so sure. James's cousin Fred, your second cousin, has been saying things that hint that as soon as Uncle Chester dies, he's going to insist that the land be cut up and sold."

"Why wait until Uncle Chester dies?"

Mama explained patiently. "Because Uncle Chester is the last of Josiah's original children. As long as he lives, those thousand acres are in his hands. Fred knows that Uncle Chester can't allow the land to be sold. That is why Agatha is trying to get Uncle Chester to give her power of attorney so she can form the land company and incorporate it *before* Chester dies."

"So what's the hang-up?"

"Uncle Chester will have none of it." Mama laughed. "Agatha just told me Uncle Chester hasn't eaten anything in two days. Swears he's not going to eat another mouthful until she forgets about getting him to sign the power of attorney papers."

"Tell Cousin Agatha to pretend that she's forgotten about the papers until Uncle Chester has eaten."

"Agatha tried that. But Uncle Chester doesn't trust her. He insists that she gives him those papers so that he can tear them up himself. He thinks that will be the end of it. And he can be a stubborn old man when he wants to be."

"Why doesn't Cousin Agatha call Cousin Gertrude? After all, Gertrude works at the hospital—she should know how to handle old people."

Mama shook her head and didn't reply. I could see that the possibility of yet another unpleasant squabble over land worried her. The one with Nat Mixon was surely unpleasant enough.

I took a deep breath. "Mama, to be honest, I'm really not in the mood for Uncle Chester right now," I said, thinking of how much I wanted to be with Cliff.

Mama frowned. "Agatha needs help. Your daddy's uncle can be a handful!"

I waved my hands submissively. Mama had that look that told me it was useless to argue with her; she had already made up her mind. We were going out in the country to help Cousin Agatha get something into my obstinate great-uncle's stomach before he starved himself to death in order to get his way. "Okay," I relented. "Let me just change my clothes. I'd feel better force-feeding Uncle Chester dressed in a jogging outfit rather than this suit."

A smile creased Mama's face as if a thought just occurred to her. "Maybe he'll eat some of my lamb stew," she said.

CHAPTER
FOUR

Daddy's cousin Agatha and her father Uncle Chester live in Nixville near the Cypress Creek Cemetery. To get to their house, you have to drive through a hollow, a long, dark, low area with cypress, gum, and pine trees hanging over the road. There is always a dense fog in Nixville, and I can always smell rotten vegetation no matter what the weather.

It was dusk when we left Otis. Thirty minutes later, we arrived at Uncle Chester's house. The full moon stood watching over the barren soybean fields like a giant orange pumpkin. A brilliant sea of white stars flashed in the sky, blinking down through the darkness.

Uncle Chester's house is a small wooden

frame building with four rooms. Still, it has character. It's surrounded by a virgin forest of pines that is filled with squirrels, deer, and foxes. The house has been patched for over fifty years and not one piece of new lumber had ever been placed on it. As we drove up in the front yard, the shadow of some large animal streaked past the car. Involuntarily, I gasped. "What was that?" I asked Mama.

"I didn't see anything," she said, turning off the engine and opening her door. She scooped up the bowl of lamb stew she'd brought.

"Now I know why I live in Atlanta," I grumbled. "The wildlife there moves on two legs."

Mama laughed as I followed her up the sagging wooden steps, onto the front porch, and into the house.

Uncle Chester's front room has a potbellied woodstove. Tonight the stove was brimming with oak wood. A kettle of water was boiling furiously on it. The whole place smelled like warm castor oil. In one corner, a large electric heater glowed.

Uncle Chester, gap-toothed, with hair sprouting from his ears, slumped in a recliner, wrapped up in a homemade quilt. Somebody had cut off a woman's stocking, tied a knot on its top, and pulled it down on his head like a bizarre cap. His eyes were deeply sunken in their sockets, his complexion a leathery mahogany with folds of skin hanging loosely under his chin and ears. He looked a hundred years old. Maybe older.

Cousin Agatha rushed forward to greet us. My second cousin is an extremely tall, extremely thin woman. Her hair is white as snow and her complexion is the color of overripe bananas full of brown spots. She always covers her mouth shyly with her hand whenever she speaks. But Cousin Agatha's timid appearance is deceiving: Agatha is extremely smart, good with figures, and handles all the Covington family's property with the canny astuteness of a business major. Agatha is the oldest daughter of Uncle Chester's first wife: He's buried three. Cousin Agatha never married, and as far as I know, never aspired to. She seemed to enjoy staying home, keeping house, taking care of her father and the heirs' property, property that has been in our family since Reconstruction.

Uncle Chester never appreciated her, has indeed always taken his daughter for granted, but it doesn't bother Cousin Agatha. The rest of the family isn't so naive, however. We know that if it hadn't been for Cousin Agatha, Uncle Chester would have been dead a long time ago and the family's property would have been sold for the taxes a dozen times over.

Within minutes of our arrival, the odor of castor oil was supplanted by the scent of Mama's lamb stew. Needless to say, I was glad. I could stop taking deep breaths and holding them.

It took Uncle Chester a while to smell the difference, however. "What you got there?" he demanded shrilly when his nose finally detected the stew above the pungent castor oil and medicines.

Mama looked as if she didn't know what he was talking about. "Where?" she asked innocently.

He pointed a very long bony finger. "What you got on top that stove?"

"Nothing," Mama replied.

A coughing sound came from somewhere deep inside Uncle Chester's sunken chest. " 'Tis something," he finally said when it cleared. He tucked his pointing finger underneath the quilt. "Don't play crazy with me, Grace Covington!"

I unsuccessfully stifled a giggle.

"That's lamb stew," Mama told him.

"Fresh?" he asked suspiciously.

"Made it this afternoon."

"What James said about it?" Uncle Chester demanded.

Mama shrugged her shoulders. "James ain't had it yet."

"Might be poison," Uncle Chester grumbled.

Mama's eyebrow shot upward. "When did you ever know me to cook up poison?"

"I hear tell there somebody poisoning people around your place," Uncle Chester insisted. His beady dark eyes were malicious. "Times has changed," he snapped. "In my day, a person want to kill another person, he knocked him on the head."

"People still get knocked in the head."

"You know what the Bible says, you reap what you sow," Uncle Chester declared.

"Yes."

"People ought to live right if they want to die right."

"I agree."

"It ain't right to profit from somebody else's killing. Lord remembers them kind of things when it's time to die!"

"You're right," Mama told him cheerfully.

Uncle Chester sat up in his chair, his eyes glued on the potbellied stove. "You ain't poisoned that there stew, now have you, Candi Covington?"

Mama shook her head. "What kind of poison would I put into my food?"

Uncle Chester's gleaming dark eyes narrowed. "What I know, poison is poison." He glared at Mama.

"Well, you ain't got to worry about me poisoning you," Mama said, crossing her arms under her breast. " 'Cause you ain't going to eat my stew, now are you?"

Uncle Chester took the challenge. "Who said I ain't?" he demanded angrily.

Mama unfolded her arms, pointed at Cousin Agatha, who had seated herself silently in the corner closest to the heater. "Agatha told me that you said you ain't up for eating until—"

"Don't pay no attention to Agatha," Uncle Chester interrupted obstinately. "I ain't never paid no attention to her, now have I?" he said triumphantly.

I burst out laughing, then hastily tried to muffle it. Uncle Chester glared at me. "What's ailing *you*?" he shrilled.

"Nothing," I said. "Nothing at all!"

He turned back to Mama. "Let me taste what you've got in that pot," he ordered. "See what you done put together for stew!"

Cousin Agatha got up, silently went into the next room, and came back with a blue bowl and a spoon. She ladled the stew into the bowl and handed the bowl to Mama. In less than ten minutes Mama had fed Uncle Chester every spoonful.

When he'd finished, he leaned back in his chair, still tucked warmly in his quilt. "Bring me more," he commanded.

Mama smiled. "I'll fix a pot especially for you and bring it later in the week," she promised.

Cousin Agatha smiled and nodded, too. But I doubted Uncle Chester saw her. He was snoring soundly.

"Uncle Chester sounds so alert and intelligent," I said to Mama as we drove back to Otis. "If it wasn't for his old body, you'd never believe he was over ninety!"

"That's because the mind doesn't age as fast as the body," Mama said reflectively. "As the years pass, Simone, the chasm between what the mind wants to do and what the body can do grows, until the gap becomes so wide it can't be bridged. That's when you realize how many years have passed!"

"I can't imagine you and Daddy being that old," I said.

Mama smiled. "Time and life catch up with everybody, honey."

The thought of my parents growing old and dying reminded me of when I was a little girl. I used to pray every night that I'd die before they did; I didn't want them to leave me.

Mama must have read my mind. "Death is not something you prepare for, Simone, it's something you accept."

It was after eight-thirty when we pulled onto Highway 633 and crossed Tenth Street. We crossed the railroad track in darkness lit by the enormous orange moon overhead and a half mile later turned off onto Smalls Lane. When we stepped out of the Honda, the cold autumn air pushed me to walk quickly into the house, but Mama hesitated. Her ebony eyes seemed glued to Miss Hannah's house next door. "Shh!" Mama whispered, holding her finger to her lips. "Listen!"

I stopped, and strained to hear the sound that had caught her attention.

It came again, this time loud and quite distinct in the evening hush. A sharp snap, as if a twig had broken under a shoe. Then another twig snapped. A bush rustled.

We stared at the spot where the noises were coming from—a bush near the foot of an old oak tree. The oak shook and leaves fell. The tree seemed to tremble as if something shook its trunk.

"Who is that!" Mama shouted. I jumped.

There was another sound. Then two huge German shepherds pushed their way through the brush in front of us. They glared at us. They growled.

Mama rolled her eyes heavenward and stood her ground. But I wasn't so courageous. My heart pounded as I grabbed her arm and pulled her toward our porch. As quickly as I could get the key turned in the lock, I pushed her into our house.

Mama and I sat at the kitchen table, drinking chocolate almond coffee and reliving my fear. "You should have seen your face." Mama laughed.

"I was scared," I said. "Okay?"

"You were *terrified*!"

"Who knows who or what could have been in those bushes?"

"Simone, you're right. There could have been *three* dogs instead of the two!"

"Yeah, right," I muttered, about the same time as my father put his key into the door.

"What's the security alarm doing turned off?" he said, by way of greeting. Daddy is a firm believer in the security alarm. There had been a few burglaries even in peaceful Otis over the past few years.

"Thank God it was turned off," I whispered, thinking of how much harder it would have been for us to get into the house and away from those nasty dogs.

"We went out and forgot to put it on when we returned," Mama told him.

"Where did you go?" Daddy asked.

"Uncle Chester's house," I answered somewhat sharply, annoyed at the habit my father had of wanting to know your every movement.

Daddy scowled.

"Your cousin Agatha called," Mama explained, her tone still light. "Your uncle stopped eating again."

"I don't know why Agatha worries about Uncle Chester. I've told her more than once, when he gets hungry he'll eat," Daddy said, his voice louder than it needed to be.

"He hadn't eaten for two days," I said.

Daddy scowled. "Don't you believe that. I'm willing to put good money on Uncle Chester having food stored away. He's just *making* Agatha think he's starving."

I laughed. "Is he that cantankerous?"

Daddy didn't answer. When he stumbled toward the table, I exclaimed, "Watch out!"

"I'm okay," he snapped.

"James," Mama said, a protective tone in her voice, "I'll fix you a cup of black coffee."

Daddy lowered himself onto the chair very carefully, perching on the edge of the seat. "I appreciate that, Candi," he said, smiling thinly.

"And you'd better check to see why that floor is so slippery."

"Remember, Mama," I said, eyeing Daddy, "we have to go next door to look for that envelope."

"You ain't got that envelope yet?" There was more sarcasm in Daddy's voice than I thought necessary.

Mama poured him a cup of steaming black coffee. "Simone wanted to wait until you could go with us," she told him. "In case there are dogs." She started to laugh.

I cut in. "In case Nat comes home and finds us," I corrected. "He's got a healthy respect for you, Daddy."

"He doesn't want me to get his behind in a sling," Daddy said.

"I'd feel better if you were with us," I told him. "Maybe tomorrow night!"

"You're leaving tomorrow," Mama reminded me.

"Oh, yeah," I said.

Daddy glanced up at the clock. "What's wrong with now?" he asked.

"I don't like the way you're moving around," I said.

"Let me get some coffee in me, that's all I need. Right, Candi?"

It was past ten when my parents and I slipped through the freezing November darkness toward the Mixon house. We were less than a hundred feet from Miss Hannah's front door when we heard a barking dog, and then the sound of a door slamming. "Mr. Brown has taken his dogs inside," Mama whispered.

We hurried to the darkened house. As Mama had predicted, we didn't need a key. Daddy pushed the unlocked door open and turned on the lights.

The little house smelled of rotten fish mixed with beer and cigarettes. Things were thrown about, stacks of newspapers, cans, and cigarette cartons. Piles of dirty clothes mounded in each corner of the sparsely furnished rooms. Mama shook her head in disappointment; Nat had already begun selling everything, I thought.

"Let's go to the bedroom. I want to get this over with," Mama said, motioning me to follow.

Miss Hannah's bedroom was practically empty. There was a double-sized square of clean carpet where the bed had once stood. The curtains were still up, but you could see light spaces on the wallpaper where pictures had hung.

We spent the next few minutes searching every nook and cranny of the one closet in the room, looking for personal papers, notes, letters, telephone numbers, a diary, or an address book. We found nothing. Nothing resembling the envelope Miss Hannah had told Calvin Stokes about.

Mama looked disappointed. She started for the bedroom door and was about to open it when she stopped. A broom leaned against the wall, a dustpan was upright beside it, and in the shadows sat a small green footlocker.

I took the broom and swept the cigarette butts and crumpled packs of empty Marlboro Lights in a pile. Mama opened the lid of the footlocker.

"Look at this," she said to me. Her voice was excited.

Given the chaos of the house in which we found it, the trunk's interior was surprisingly tidy. On the left, neatly folded and stacked, bath towels were beautifully monogrammed with Miss Hannah's initials. Beneath the towels were sheets that had little pink roses on them. On the right-hand side lay an old Bible.

Hannah Mixon's name was on the flyleaf. Mama flipped through the book and found a folded-up sheet of paper tucked into its back. The crude map was a diagram of a farm. It showed where a barn was supposed to be, a machine shed, a grain bin, and fields. Paper-clipped to the diagram's top right-hand corner was a photograph of an old house.

Mama refolded the map and slipped it back into the Bible. "I'm taking this with me," she said. Tucking the Bible under her arm, she motioned me to follow her out of the room.

Daddy was leaning against the front door, waiting for us. "No envelope?" he asked.

Mama shook her head. "Nothing but this Bible."

Daddy walked to the front door and held it open. He yawned. Daddy never found Mama's sleuthing very exciting.

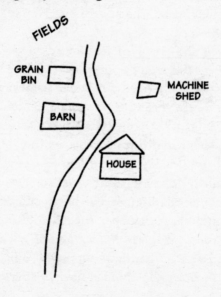

When we stepped out of Miss Hannah's house, I had the sudden odd sensation that someone was watching us. To my left, toward the back of the Mixon's house, I thought I saw a flicker of movement, a shadow. I turned quickly to look. Nothing.

But as we walked across the darkness of the yard, the feeling that we were being observed intensified. Again, I looked around. Nothing, nothing at all! The street was empty. No loose dogs. No cars. Not even a winter breeze rustled the trees. Still, I felt my hair rising up along my scalp.

I touched Mama's arm. "Do you feel like we're being watched?" I whispered.

Mama's eyes were scanning the area. She nodded.

"You do?" I exclaimed, satisfied that for once I wasn't being paranoid about dogs.

"Yeah," she answered, softly. And from out of nowhere, a chill swept down the empty street.

Ahead of us, Daddy kept walking home, but Mama and I stopped and stared out into the darkness. There were no signs of life. The widely spaced streetlights created shallow pools of wan illumination that served only to heighten the impenetrable shadows in between. Ever so faintly in the darkness I thought I picked up a sharp tap, but neither Daddy nor Mama seem to notice.

Daddy motioned us forward, impatient with our nervousness. We hurried after him. Still, when I closed our front door safely behind us, I could feel the unseen presence outside like a cold wave, something chilly and secretive.

I headed for the kitchen immediately. Coffee was definitely in order. The message light on the answering machine was blinking. Daddy pressed the playback button.

"James, Candi, this is Agatha," an anxious voice stammered. *"Uncle Chester is sick. The ambulance has taken him to Otis General Hospital!"*

CHAPTER
FIVE

"Where is Hannah's Bible?" Mama shouted.

My eyes snapped open. I jerked upright.

"I put it on the desk in the kitchen," Mama continued loudly. "Simone, did you move it?" My mother was standing at my bedroom door, her face stern, her hands folded across her chest like a drill sergeant. I was groggy, but I could see that she was fully dressed. She had on a calf-length skirt, a sweater, and her fuzzy pink bedroom slippers.

I closed my eyes and swore.

"Simone!" Mama hollered in a tone intended to do more than grab my attention.

I yawned, then reluctantly reopened my eyes.

"After last night, I can't believe you're up looking for an old Bible!" I grumbled. I had slept badly and I was certain my parents had, too. We'd only gotten home from the hospital three hours earlier. Uncle Chester's doctor had told us that Uncle Chester had had a heart attack, a mild one. His condition had become stable and he probably would be leaving the hospital sometime later in the week.

"I've got to find that Bible," Mama insisted.

"Mama, I don't know where you put it," I murmured.

"Simone, I need to find it—*now,*" she snapped.

I burrowed back under the covers. What I really needed was six more hours of sleep: There was no way I was going to get out of bed and hunt for an old Bible belonging to a dead woman at this time of the morning. "Why don't you go to bed and look for it when it gets daylight?" I muttered into the soft warmth of my pillow.

"Get up and help me find it," Mama insisted.

"If I get up now, I'm going straight back to Atlanta," I threatened.

"Get——up!" Mama roared.

I tried thinking of something to say that would get her out of my room. I couldn't.

"Now!" Mama snapped, then swung out of

the room and sashayed down the hall toward her kitchen.

I fell back down and pulled the covers up to my chin. Ignore her, I thought. Pretend that she's still asleep. I enjoyed a very few minutes of this fantasy before Mama bellowed: *"Simone!"*

I sat up again and glanced at the bedside clock. It was six-fifteen A.M., still dark outside. The clock ticked. I watched the hands move. I could hear Mama pushing and pulling things in the kitchen, I could smell the Irish-cream coffee. The dial moved to six-nineteen. I rolled over, picked up the phone, and called Cliff at his hotel in New York City.

"Something the matter?" he asked once he was sure it was me and not some lunatic making a crank call at the crack of dawn.

"Are you coming home today?" I asked.

"Sorry, baby," he said between yawns. "Not only are things not getting better, they are getting worse!"

I groaned. Why did Cliff always get the crazy clients? "What is Mrs. Zwig up to now?" I asked.

"The Zwigs are determined to destroy each other." He sighed. "I'm going to meet with Mr. Zwig's lawyer this afternoon, try to bring some reasonableness into this mess."

"I might as well stay here in Otis another

day," I said, but I can't say that I said it too cheerfully.

"How are things going there?"

"Mama is trying to get rid of two hundred and fifty acres of land one of her neighbors willed her."

"Must be nice," Cliff said.

"Not if the neighbor who left it to her was murdered."

"Don't tell me Miss Candi has got another murder to investigate," Cliff said.

"Yeah," I grumbled, "and she woke me up ten minutes ago hollering about some Bible we found at the dead woman's house."

"Then you're not lonely," Cliff said. "Miss Candi's keeping you busy and I don't believe you miss me at all—"

"Don't even try it!"

"Simone!" Mama's voice blasted again.

I cringed. "Can you hear her calling me?" I asked Cliff.

He laughed. "Yes, but I bet she'd die if she knew it."

I put my hand over the telephone receiver. "Mama, Cliff said he heard your voice and he wants me to tell you good morning!" I shouted.

Nothing.

"She knows now," I told him, smugly.

"That was mean," he said.

"*Mean* is waking me up at six o'clock A.M. when I got only in bed three hours earlier."

"What on earth were you doing up at three o'clock in the morning?"

"Daddy's uncle got sick. We had to go to the hospital."

"Anything serious?"

"For a ninety-nine-year-old man, everything is serious. But Uncle Chester is no ordinary old man. He's going to be fine."

"You'd better help Miss Candi. Sounds like she's got her hands full!"

"Mama can handle it," I replied. "When she's doing her thing, she positively thrives on three hours of sleep."

"Still . . ." he said.

I stretched. "Oh, I'll help her. But believe me, she'll pay."

Cliff chuckled. "Blackmail?"

"She'll have to make my favorite breakfast. . . ."

"Now, Simone, don't be naughty."

"You don't know what naughty is," I said, flirting. "If you ever break away from your vengeful client and get back to Atlanta, you'll see how naughty your Simone can be."

"Is that a threat or a promise?"

"Both."

"In that case, I'll do everything I can to get to

Atlanta. And you'd better believe I'm holding you to your threat. And your promise."

Minutes later, I reluctantly put the phone on its receiver, wrapped my white terry-cloth robe loosely around me, and padded barefoot into Mama's kitchen.

"Cliff said to tell you hello," I said.

Mama was wiping her hands on her apron and leaning back against the counter. She'd just poured herself a cup of coffee. There was a troubled look in her eyes.

She shook her head. "I'm sorry. I shouldn't have waked you like that. But it concerns me that I can't find Hannah's Bible!"

I moved closer to my mother. Or should I say closer to the coffeepot that sat on the counter beside her? The scent of coffee was tantalizing, even in my groggy condition. I gave Mama a hug. "Do you have to have that Bible this minute?" I asked.

"James says he didn't move it. If you haven't touched it, Simone, it means that . . ."

I yawned, reached for a mug, and poured myself a cup of coffee. Mama found mysteries everywhere. "It means that it's where you put it!"

Mama pulled out a chair and sat down at the

table. "Simone, that Bible is no place in this house!"

I joined her at the table. After a few hot, rich sips from my cup, I felt strong enough to speak. "Mama, I'm tired and you should be, too. Can't Miss Hannah's Bible wait?"

Her eyes stayed obstinate.

"I'll make a deal with you," I teased.

"You're being silly, and this isn't the time for it!" she said.

I grinned. "If you be a nice little mama and go to bed and let me get some sleep, I'll help you search for that Bible when I wake up, I promise!"

Mama frowned. "I'm not tired and I don't expect to get much sleep until I've found why Hannah Mixon left me those two hundred and fifty acres."

I rubbed my forehead and sighed. I should have known better than to talk Mama out of something once she'd made her mind up.

"Okay, okay," I told her. "Since you're not going to let me get any sleep, you'll have to cook breakfast. After I've eaten, I promise to help you look for the Bible."

"I thought you were going home this morning. You can get breakfast at Hardee's."

The thought of eating fast food when I could get Mama's cooking was sickening. "Cliff can't get back to Atlanta, so I'll stay and help you find Miss Hannah's Bible. But only if—"

Mama cleared her throat. Then she pushed back her chair and stood up. "You think you're smart, don't you? How many times have I told you not to try to manipulate me into doing what you want me to do?"

I grinned. "I don't know what you're talking about," I lied.

"Yeah, right," Mama grumbled, opening the refrigerator door and carefully choosing two large eggs.

I took another sip from my cup. The coffee was heavenly and suddenly I was starving. "I want eggs, toast, grits, sausage," I told her. Blackmail could be fun.

Mama pulled an unopened package of Quaker Grits from the cupboard. She didn't say another word. For the next twenty minutes, despite the tension in her face, she concentrated on doing her thing, turning food from the simple to the gourmet.

I suppose I should feel guilty, eating Mama's food and not offering to help her. The fact is that watching Mama cook gives me a special comfort. It takes me back to when I was six years old, sitting waiting for something special to come out of her oven. It's a feeling that I only get when

I'm in Mama's kitchen, when she's working her magic just for me!

By the time Mama had finished cooking, Daddy had gotten out of bed, showered, and joined us. He was wearing a pair of old jeans, a long-sleeved cotton knit shirt, and a pair of brown leather boots that Cliff had picked out for him. He didn't say a word about how early we were up. He was well into his breakfast, eating a second helping of sausage, when Mama asked him about what was really on her mind.

"James, are you sure you didn't move Hannah's Bible?" she asked.

Daddy shook his head, winced, and stuffed his mouth full of scrambled eggs all at about the same time. "Like I told you when we came in this morning," he said after he swallowed and washed the whole thing down with orange juice, "the last time I laid eyes on that Bible was when I saw you put it on that table over there!" He pointed toward the small desk that held the telephone.

"I know it was there when we left the house," Mama insisted. She was pushing her food around her plate in some kind of pattern. "Still . . ."

Daddy fixed his eyes on her, looking down his nose in a kind of "for God's sake not now" manner that he uses when he doesn't want Mama to lay anything heavy on him. "What's on your mind, Candi?" he asked.

Mama sat upright, folded her hands in her lap. Their eyes met. "James, is it possible that somebody came into this house last night when we went to the hospital to see about Uncle Chester?"

"The alarm—" I began.

Daddy started to say something, too. That's when we all heard a noise at the back of the house. I looked toward the window. Outside, the dawn was gray and heavy. Then we heard the noise again. I think the realization that somebody was trying to break into our house hit all three of us at the same time.

I started for the phone, but Daddy motioned me not to touch it. He pushed back his chair, walked to the hall closet, and pulled out his gun; he inserted a clip.

Mama and I followed him down the hallway. I was amazed at his calmness. Without looking the least bit worried, he moved to the entrance of our darkened living room, his gun cocked. He cleared his throat as if to alert the intruder that he was approaching. Silence. He walked into the room and disappeared from view; the only sound I heard was the ticking of the antique clock on the mantel that had once belonged to Josiah Covington. Then Daddy switched on the lights;

the living room was empty. Still holding his gun, he walked down the hall toward the bedrooms. Again Mama followed. And not wanting to be left alone, I hurried after her. Daddy stopped at their bedroom door and again cleared his throat. Silence. He nudged their door open, stepped inside and turned on the ceiling light; no one was there. He turned on their bathroom light. That room, too, was empty.

Both Mama and I were so close behind him that when he turned quickly he knocked over a blue-and-white flowerpot that sat in the bathroom window. When I put the pot back, I glimpsed movement outside in the shadows. The next second, before I had time to warn Daddy, I heard the tap on the pane. Someone was standing outside of *my* bedroom window. I gasped.

My father walked unhurriedly to my bedroom door. He motioned us to stand back. He opened the door once again and disappeared into the darkness. My heart pounded. Beside me, Mama stood absolutely still. Another tap. I heard Daddy inch forward.

"Simone! Simone!" the person outside called in a raspy whisper. The voice was unmistakable; it belonged to Nat Mixon.

Daddy turned on the light and moved quickly to the window. "For God's sake, Nat, what are you doing out there in the freezing cold?" he demanded angrily. "What's the matter with you?"

"Help me!" Nat hollered.

"Go to the kitchen door," Daddy yelled back. Nat turned away.

Moments later, Mama flung open the door. Then she gasped. The smell of the blood and salty sweat that was pouring into Nat's eyes was strong.

"My Lord," Mama whispered, moving forward to help him inside. Mama can't bear to see anything or anyone suffer.

Daddy wasn't so kindhearted. "Boy, are you crazy? What's the matter with you, sneaking around Simone's window this early in the morning?"

"Somebody tried to kill me!" Nat cried.

"*I* almost killed you," Daddy pointed out gruffly, putting his gun back in the closet.

"Somebody hit me on my head with a hammer!" Nat spoke as if the shock and horror suddenly dawned upon him. "He tried to *kill me!*" he insisted through bloody spit.

"Are you dizzy?" Daddy asked. "Is your vision okay?"

Nat gasped. Then, as if the pain in his head had lanced all the way into his body, he began gagging.

"Get a bucket," Daddy ordered me.

I ran into the bathroom, grabbed Mama's foot tub, and brought it back just in time.

"You strong enough to make it to the hospital?" Daddy asked, when the last wrenching spasm had shuddered through Nat's skinny body.

Nat tried to nod. But the motion made him gag again. Blood dripped from his nose and mouth. He looked dreadful. "We can't wait," Daddy told us. "Candi, you'll have to hold the bucket. Simone, take the keys from my pocket. You drive."

"I'm not dressed," I protested.

Daddy braced Nat against his shoulder and lifted him out of the chair as if he were a child. "Then it's you and me, Candi," he said. "We've got to get this boy to the hospital *now*!"

Nat blinked. "I-I can't see," he choked. "I can't." He sounded like he couldn't believe what was happening to him.

"It'll soon be all right, once we get you to the hospital," Daddy told him.

"Wait!" Mama put the bucket on the floor, ran to the hall closet, and brought out coats. She tucked one around Nat, one around Daddy. She threw her fuzzy pink slippers into a corner, trading them for a pair of boots.

"M-my eyes hurt," Nat whimpered.

"Take it easy, boy," Daddy told him. "We'll

have you to the hospital directly. There's nothing to worry about, son!" He no longer sounded angry. Instead, he sounded very worried.

I joined my parents in Otis General Hospital Emergency Room for the second time in less than twelve hours. When I walked in, Nat was in a bed, his bandaged head propped up higher than the rest of his body. He looked so defenseless. Now I understood what Mama had said earlier. Nat really was a lost child who needed someone to take care of him.

Daddy was talking to Dr. Jamison, the same doctor who had examined Uncle Chester last night. The doctor's thick black curly hair seemed to sparkle in the bright hospital light. "I'm going to have him admitted," the doctor told Daddy. "He has a concussion, you know. You got him to the hospital quick, that's good!"

Daddy nodded grimly. "I did what I had to do."

The doctor took out a small white pad and pencil. "Tell me, what happened to the young man?" he asked.

Daddy shook his head. "I don't know. I didn't take time to ask him."

"You don't know who hit him so brutally?" The doctor frowned.

Daddy tucked his hands in his pockets, a gesture he uses when he feels tense but is trying to fake it. "No," he said brusquely.

The doctor looked him directly in the eyes. "Police will want to know," he said.

Daddy's eyes didn't blink. "Then they'll have to get the story from Nat," he said. "When he came to our house, he had already gotten busted."

The doctor looked confused. He slipped his little pad back in his pocket. "I'll have to tell the police you brought him here," he said.

Daddy's hands slipped further into his pockets. "Tell the police anything you want. My wife and daughter were with me having breakfast, Nat started banging on the window, we opened it, and," he pointed to Nat, who was moaning softly while Mama held his hand, "this is what we found."

Dr. Jamison smiled and nodded politely, as if he didn't quite believe Daddy's story but was too courteous to dispute it. "Thanks very much," he murmured, then turned and walked away quickly down the long white corridor.

"You're going to be all right," I whispered to Nat. He looked at me, then closed his eyes. A tear rolled down his bruised face. His lips quivered and I imagined he was praying that his dead mother would come walking through the door and protect him from all the world's misery.

Ten minutes later, my parents and I were in their car underneath the stoplight on King Street. Mama shook her head. "Nothing about this whole thing makes sense to me," she said. "Who would want to hurt Nat like that?"

"The secret to this mess is in that envelope," I said. "Once we find it, we'll find Miss Hannah's murderer, and maybe—"

Mama cut in before I could finish my sentence. "And maybe save her darn fool son's life!" she said softly.

CHAPTER
SIX

My parents had taken the previous day off to keep their appointment with the lawyer Calvin Stokes. Today they both went to work, Mama to the welfare office and Daddy to Westinghouse, Micarta Division.

I was alone in the house, but I couldn't seem to settle down. The weather was cold, the November sky gray, heavy with icy rain. Inside was warm but, for some reason, it too felt as depressing as the outdoors.

Of course, I missed Cliff. I cursed the fighting Zwigs whom I hoped never to meet, and I cursed Mr. Zwig's live-in secretary for getting herself pregnant. It's not fair, I thought. These people who don't even know I exist shouldn't impact my life.

For the twentieth time that morning, I glanced through the window at the little house next door, the house where Hannah Mixon had lived and where she had died. Smalls Lane is a cul-de-sac. Besides my parents' house and Hannah and Nat Mixon's, there are four other houses on Smalls Lane. Each has a large yard planted with oak and magnolia trees. Behind Smalls Lane is a patch of woods that is a mile deep. On the other side of those woods a highway leads to Highway 6, the road that takes you to Darien.

Miss Hannah's house is cement block. It had originally been painted white and green. Now, its exterior was faded, its awnings dirty. Everything about the house needed repair. It was a shabby sight, as dreary as the weather.

On the other hand, my parents' home is a sprawling brick ranch with huge, bright rooms that are filled with objects from Daddy's tours around the world. Daddy had purchased this property years earlier when they were first married, before my two brothers and I were born. I suspected that, even back then, Daddy planned to build on it whenever he retired. He always intended to call Otis home, no matter where the Air Force took him.

I sighed. Otis seemed so peaceful. Why would anybody who lived here poison Miss Hannah? Why would someone try to kill Nat? It was true that Miss Hannah was hateful, but as far as I could tell that was her only sin. And Nat, poor Nat, a thirty-year-old uneducated man whose only errors seemed to be that he was never trained to do anything productive and that he couldn't seem to hang on to a dime. It was true, Nat probably owed everybody in Otis money. Last year, he'd borrowed twenty dollars from me, which, now that I think of it, he never paid back. Could the attack on him last night have something to do with his bad habit of borrowing money? Maybe, I thought, he owed someone a lot of money and that person had murdered his mother, thinking that Nat could repay him back with Hannah's insurance money.

As a paralegal, I decided, I'd been trained to dig, to find a trail and follow it. I sat down with a notepad to jot down questions that I intended to find answers to. On the top of one page I put down, MISS HANNAH: *At least 60 years old. Married at least twice. She must have had Nat when she was 30. Check into her past . . . her husbands . . . her relatives . . . check county tax records to see when she bought the 250 acres of land . . . find envelope . . . Find Bible!*

On the next page, I wrote, NAT: *Thirty, uned-*

ucated, loves to gamble, hang out at Melody Bar.
Check into his friends . . . his girlfriends . . .
people he owes money.

Anything else? I wondered as I fidgeted with my pencil. Nothing came to mind. I picked up the remote and clicked on the television. A talk show had a mother and daughter who had switched roles. That was as senseless, I thought, as a murderer being a part of the serene Otis community. I clicked off the remote.

Next I checked out Mama's bookshelves. She had a collection of books that she had gotten from the places where she and my father traveled. I found one that interested me. I curled up on the sofa and read until I fell asleep.

Around three o'clock I was up again wandering around the house. Lunch had been a thick ham sandwich and a cup of hot tea with lemon. I was sitting with my notepad again, trying to figure out a motive for Miss Hannah's murder, when the doorbell rang. Surprised, because I didn't expect a visitor, I disarmed the alarm system and opened the front door to find Sarah Jenkins, Annie Mae Gregory, and Carrie Smalls standing on Mama's doorstep.

"Thank goodness you're home," Carrie Smalls said, pulling at the front door to escape wind and rain.

"Ladies," I said, ushering them into the dry, warm house. I closed the door behind them.

Annie Mae Gregory is a huge, dark woman. Her black eyes are small and very piercing—in her fat face, her eyes always remind me of a raccoon's. She has small black moles on each side of her face that extend from her bottom eyelid down to her neck. When her head is tilted a certain way, Annie Mae looks a little cross-eyed.

Sarah Jenkins, on the other hand, is a tiny, frail-looking woman with a pecan complexion that's filled with wrinkles. Mama has told me that Sarah Jenkins is obsessed with her own health and visits her doctor's office at least once a week. Today, she smelled sour, like vinegar and garlic.

Carrie Smalls is very tall, with mocha-colored skin and long straight hair that hangs to her shoulders. She looks younger than the other ladies but, I believe, that's because she dyes her hair an extraordinary shade of jet black. Carrie Smalls has a strong chin, thin lips, and eyes that seldom seem to blink. She has a strength about her. It's Carrie Smalls's strength that gives the three women their presence when they are together. And when they're together, you know gossip is on the menu.

"We came over to ask you what happened to

Nat Mixon early this morning," Carrie Smalls began, her intense eyes locked on my face.

My mouth opened, but nothing came out. For a moment, I really didn't know what to say. I finally stammered, "Would you ladies like a cup of tea?"

"Lord, yes," Sarah Jenkins exclaimed, wrapping her neck with a thick scarf of navy wool. "Dr. Clark told me yesterday to stay in out of this weather, what with my various ailments."

Annie Mae and Carrie decided they would like tea, too.

After I hung up each of the ladies' coats in the hall closet, I directed them into the kitchen. Once I had them seated and had turned on the teakettle, Annie Mae Gregory opened the conversation. "Simone, we got news that somebody hit Nat Mixon over the head." Her jowls shook as she spoke.

"Yes," I said, my mind wild in trying to figure out how to handle this. Mama held that these three women knew useful information. You could say Carrie, Sarah, and Annie Mae were the town's historians—they knew everything about everybody in Otis.

Sarah Jenkins took out a handkerchief and blew her nose. "Your Mama and Daddy took Nat to the hospital just after daylight," she said.

I took cups and saucers from the cupboard, all

the while wondering how these women had learned so much in such a short time. The FBI could use their skills, I thought, and tried not to giggle. "What can I tell you?" I said.

Carrie Smalls tilted her head upward. "Tell us whether or not you saw anybody hanging around Nat's house, anybody who would try to kill the boy?"

I was speechless. "No," I said, at last. Then I decided that this wasn't my expertise. "Maybe you ladies would enjoy your visit more if Mama was here," I said, reaching for the telephone and dialing Mama's office number. "Maybe she could come home."

"We tried to see Candi," Sarah Jenkins said. "We stopped by the welfare office before we came here. Candi was busy, she wouldn't see us."

"She was talking to that womanish Tippy Turner," Annie Mae Gregory said. "That girl's carrying her third child, and ain't about to marry that good-for-nothing boyfriend of hers."

"Maybe Mama is free now," I suggested, waiting for the receptionist to answer the phone. After a moment, Mama was on the other end of the line. "Mama," I began, "Sarah Jenkins, Annie Mae Gregory, and Carrie Smalls stopped for a visit and—"

"She's coming home?" Carrie Smalls asked. Her nose twitched.

I said good-bye to Mama, who had just ordered me not to say a word, and replaced the phone. "Yes. It's only a five-minute drive from her office. Meantime, I'll fix you ladies tea and give you a piece of Mama's sweet potato pie."

The ladies had just cleaned their plates when Mama walked into the room. My mother had a look on her face that was a mixture of amazement and satisfaction. I surmised she was surprised that the women were so determined to get their information. Still, she was happy to be able to have this chat with them. "Ladies," she said, taking off her coat and laying it on a chair.

"Candi," Sarah Jenkins said, "it's so nice to see you, dear. I declare you look younger each time I see you."

"You're looking well, too, Sarah," Mama replied.

"Ain't doing good though," Sarah Jenkins said. "Dr. Clark got me on heart medicine now, you know."

"No," Mama said, shaking her head.

I wondered why a woman with a heart problem would be facing this weather just to talk about somebody else's business. But I was smart enough just to sip tea and say nothing.

Mama shook her head again. "I'm real sorry

to hear about your heart, Sarah. And I'm sorry we couldn't talk at the office, but—"

Carrie Smalls interrupted. "We would have never bothered you at your job or come here, Candi, if we weren't so worried about Nat."

"Nat is going to be all right," Mama said.

"We stopped by the hospital to see the dear boy, but he was sleeping, and James's cousin Gertrude wouldn't let us wake him," Annie Mae Gregory said.

Sarah Jenkins wrapped her hands around her bosom, pushing up her breast. "So, we came straight to you, Candi. We knew that you'd tell us how the poor boy is doing!"

"Nat is fine," Mama assured them. She sat down and motioned me to pour her a cup of tea. "You know," she said, after she was satisfied that her brew had plenty of sugar and lemon in it, "Hannah Mixon was my neighbor. I saw her as much as anybody in the area. Still, I didn't know much about her."

Carrie Smalls made a throaty sound. "That's 'cause Hannah was a selfish woman. She could live in this world alone, except for her boy, Nat."

"I never saw visitors. I wondered about her family," Mama continued serenely.

"Hannah didn't have family," Carrie Smalls stated. "Her people died before she was full grown. Course, being married so many times, she had a lot of in-laws." She said this grimly, as if in-laws were germs. I tried to remember if Carrie Smalls had ever married.

Mama cleared her throat. "Did either of you ladies know Hannah's husbands?" she asked, an innocence in her voice.

"Of course we knew them!" Annie Mae Gregory roared. "I courted her first husband, Curtis Joyner, myself. That was before Curtis ever knew Hannah. Should have married him, could have if I had wanted to. Curtis died six months after Hannah got him. Had that Spanish flu that was going around right after the war."

I cleared my throat.

"World War One," Mama explained to me, keeping her eyes on Annie Mae.

Carrie Smalls continued. "It was years later when Hannah married her second husband, Charles Warren. He wasn't half the man Curtis was. Charles was Nat's father. The boy was only a baby when Charles got himself killed in a gambling fight." Carrie Smalls shook her head. "Nat's got bad blood in him. I reckon Hannah knew it, too. That's why she didn't try to make much out of the boy."

"And her third husband?" Mama asked.

This time Annie Mae Gregory answered. "His name was Richard Wescot. Richard was from

Darien. He was a fine-looking man, a red bone, high yellow with a deep singing voice."

"He used to sing quartet," Carrie Smalls added.

"Richard had people follow him all the way to Melbourne just to hear him sing," Annie Mae Gregory agreed.

"I've seen him turn out more than one church service," Sarah Jenkins added. "Poor Richard wasn't married to Hannah for more than three years before he died."

"Miss Hannah may not have had the best personality," I declared, "but she certainly had the knack of getting married."

"Hannah got husbands but she seemed to lose them as fast," Mama pointed out.

Sarah Jenkins coughed. "I'll tell you one thing, nobody in this town was surprised when Hannah snagged her fourth husband, Leroy Mixon."

Mama looked puzzled.

Sarah Jenkins tried to laugh, but started coughing, instead. Nobody said anything until it was certain that she was going to live.

"That's because Leroy Mixon was just like Hannah," Carrie Smalls said firmly. "Together they were the meanest two people in these parts!"

That night, Nat was sitting up in his hospital bed, his long legs stretched out under the white sheet, his head wrapped neatly in bandages. Mama sat at his bedside. Daddy stood leaning at the door.

Mama urged Nat to tell me his story. Nat tilted his head to one side and gave me one of his most dejected looks. "I walked into the house—" he began.

I was impatient. "What time was that?" I interrupted.

"Five, six—"

"It had to be before six," I said. "Everybody in the world was up at six A.M., right, Mama?"

Mama cut her eyes. "Go on, Nat," she said, "tell Simone what happened next."

Nat yawned. "Somebody hit me in the back of my head," he said.

"We know that!" I said, exasperated.

Nat looked up, his head cocked. "Felt like it was with a hammer!"

Daddy interjected, "Big boy like you should watch out for falling hammers!"

"He must have hid behind something, 'cause if I'd seen him, he'd never got the best of *me*!" Nat declared.

Daddy laughed.

"Do you have any idea who it could have been?" I asked Nat.

"No," Nat said. "But he was big."

Mama's voice sounded relaxed, at ease. "Bigger than you?" she asked.

Nat took a deep, shuddering breath. "He was *big!*" he repeated.

We weren't getting very far. "Anything else?" I asked.

Nat hesitated. Then he wrinkled his nose. "He smelled funny," he told us.

Mama's eyes opened wide. "You didn't tell me that."

"*Funny?*" I asked.

"Yeah," Nat answered. He rubbed his eyes and yawned again.

"Funny like what?" Mama demanded.

"I don't know. If I smell it again, I'll tell you," Nat answered, making me long to smack him over his head myself.

"Maybe he smelled like alcohol," Daddy told Nat. "Like your favorite brew!"

It's amazing, I thought, how easily my father could see Nat's drinking as a problem but couldn't see his own.

Nat shook his head. "It was something else," he insisted. "Something I never smelled before."

"It may be a good idea for you to stay with us for a while," Mama said. Daddy frowned.

This seemed to terrify Nat. "Oh, no!" he cried, his mouth slack with panic.

"Suppose whoever hit you comes back?" Mama asked.

Nat made a gesture. "Don't worry, I'm listening to you, I'm gonna make sure that all the doors and windows are locked from now on."

"Always look behind you," Daddy joked. "Most big fellers hit from behind!"

We had left the hospital, and were back in our snug kitchen when I turned again to the window with its view of Miss Hannah's shabby little house. "Have you wondered how Miss Hannah got to own two hundred and fifty acres of prime land?" I asked Mama. "The way she and Nat lived, you'd never thought she had anything valuable."

Mama began cutting slices from a fresh loaf of wheat bread. "I don't reckon nobody knew Hannah owned that land. Except maybe the tax collector."

"I was thinking the same thing. I plan to check the county tax records tomorrow, see when she got the land."

"That's a good idea, Simone," Mama said.

Daddy sneezed loudly, pulled out his handkerchief, and wiped his nose. "Around here, land is more valuable than gold."

"It's so valuable," I said, "that your Uncle

Chester refuses to die so that he can continue to control the acres of land owned by your family."

Mama started to say something, but Daddy broke in. "Uncle Chester can't live too much longer—nobody lives forever. I've told Agatha to wait a few more months, a year at the most, and then she can do whatever she needs to do with that land."

Mama shook her head. "James, you don't understand. It's prudent to take care of the land *before* Uncle Chester dies. That way, there won't be a nasty fight among the cousins, the heirs. If Uncle Chester would only give Agatha the power of attorney, she can go ahead and set up the Covington Land Company and incorporate it. Agatha has already started the process; Calvin Stokes has drawn up the papers. The corporation would be set up for one hundred years. That way the land will stay in the family."

Daddy sneezed again. But he didn't say a word.

"Agatha has been satisfied with getting the timber cut and paying the taxes," Mama continued, "but she knows that she ain't going to be able to take care of the land forever."

"I never thought of that," I said.

"James, you and your cousins are the second generation. Agatha knows that none of the Covington children of the third generation is going to take responsibility for that land. Agatha is afraid that when she dies, the Covington property will get sold, or worse, lost for taxes."

"I wouldn't want the responsibility of handling the Covington property, of seeing that it stays in the family," I said.

Daddy scowled. "I agree with Agatha that our parents worked hard for that land. They did without a lot of things to buy it and to keep it. It'll be a shame to lose it from neglect."

Mama nodded. "Agatha is doing the right thing," she said firmly. "And somehow we've got to make Uncle Chester understand that!"

CHAPTER
SEVEN

Cliff and I talked around ten-thirty that night. He was still tied up in New York. The Zwigs were going at it tooth and nail. Needless to say, I was depressed. The thought of going back to work again in Atlanta without so much as looking into his face was sickening. And the next morning the black cloud still seemed to hang over my head. I called Sidney and begged for the balance of the week off. He quickly agreed.

Mama seemed a little preoccupied. She hadn't gotten any closer to finding either Miss Hannah's Bible or the mysterious envelope.

Around ten A.M., I set off to find the source of Miss Hannah's large property holding. I headed for the Otis County Courthouse, a large, very ugly brick building built in 1878 that sits at the head of Main Street.

It took me an hour to find the source of Hannah Mixon's large property holdings. That's because when I couldn't find a record of Miss Hannah's purchase in the Clerk of Court Deed Books, I went to Probate Court on the assumption that Miss Hannah could have inherited the land from one of her husbands. Sure enough, I found Leroy Mixon's will stating that the property would belong to Hannah Mixon and, upon her death, it would pass on to her son, Nat.

"Not anymore," I murmured, reading the fine print in the will. "Upon her death, it passed on to my Mama, Candi Covington."

Before going back to our house, I stopped into the drugstore to pick up a few candy bars. I was looking though the selection, trying to convince myself that I didn't need to buy as many as I wanted to, when I saw Sarah Jenkins, Annie Mae Gregory, and Carrie Smalls drive up outside in the large blue Buick owned and solely driven by Carrie Smalls.

I started to slip toward the back of the store, because I didn't want another encounter without Mama's presence. Fortunately, the three women didn't see me. They were too busy talking. They stopped in front of the pharmacy, their backs to me.

"Well, if you ask me," Annie Mae Gregory was saying, "Candi knows more than she's letting on." Her large body seemed to tremble with excitement.

"Hannah hated Candi, I know that for a fact," Sarah Jenkins said.

The sound of these women talking about Mama twisted something inside me.

Carrie Smalls interjected. "It's mighty suspicious that Candi was the one to take Nat to the hospital."

"Seems pretty clear to me," Annie Mae continued. "Candi might not have been doing that boy any favor dragging him to the hospital if she was the one that tried to kill him."

"Candi tries to make people think she ain't changed since she's come back home to live, but I don't buy it," Carrie Smalls said.

I was shocked, to say the least. My first impulse was to give the women a piece of my mind, to set them straight about talking about Mama. Then it occurred to me that Mama would want to know what they were saying, so I controlled my inclination and eased around on the other side of the aisle so that I could better hear their talk without them knowing I was listening.

Annie Mae Gregory spoke. "You can't travel

all over the world and mingle with different people and come back home the same way as you left."

"I dare say, Candi could have learned how to hide poison in Hannah's food when she was overseas," Sarah Jenkins said.

Annie Mae Gregory's huge body stiffened. "If Candi had something to do with Hannah's dying and somebody hitting poor Nat, she had a reason."

"Talk is that Hannah didn't like her neighbors," Sarah contributed.

"What is it she didn't like about Candi?" Carrie asked.

"Don't know exactly," Sarah Jenkins said, "but Hannah told my first cousin's wife that Candi tried to bring her something to eat once. Hannah said she knew better than to eat anything from Candi Covington's house."

"Hannah might have known something about Candi that we don't," Carrie Smalls said.

"If you ask me, Hannah suspected Candi of trying to poison her then," Annie Mae Gregory said.

That was enough. My appetite for candy was gone. I fought an impulse to slap each of the women and instead, eased toward the front door. Once in my Honda, I headed home.

I called Mama at the welfare office and told her that I'd overheard the women's conversation.

"Simone," Mama said, annoyed more than surprised, "do you know what those women will do to my reputation if they ever find out Hannah put me in her will?"

"Mama, in a few weeks *everybody* in Otis will know about that will. It will be public knowledge, recorded in the Probate just like all other wills."

For a second, Mama didn't say anything. "We've got to find Hannah's killer before that happens," she finally said. "Before those women make it impossible for me to hold up my head in this town!"

❦

On Saturday morning, Daddy and a few of his buddies left town for a hunting trip to North Carolina. I knew that would mean that Mama would be free to sleuth uninterruptedly for a few days, something I suspected she dearly wanted to do. She told me she had decided that the first thing she would do was to ask around about the unknown woman who had come with Nat the morning he'd come to our house accusing Mama of stealing his land.

I didn't talk to Cliff again until late Saturday afternoon. He had finally gotten the Affair Zwig settled. I was elated. He was flying into Harts-field in Atlanta on Sunday; he expected to arrive there around noon.

I glanced at my watch, eased my foot on the gas and drove away from my parents' home. It was early Sunday morning, just before seven. There was no rain, but a few snow flurries did fall as I drove through the Savannah River Plant into Augusta. My heart pounded and my flesh tingled. I was going to have a few hours with Cliff, a few precious hours. Nothing was going to take that away from us, I thought. Little did I know that I'd be driving back to Otis at two-forty that *same* afternoon—that's exactly what Cliff and I had to do.

This is what went down. Around eleven-thirty, I pulled into my parking space in the apartment complex where I lived on South Hairston Park-way. Atlanta was damp, the clouds gray and very low. My apartment was dark and unwelcoming, just like the weather. I turned on lights, hoping to create the illusion that things were warm and bright. I set up a pot of fresh coffee and flipped the switch, and soon the aroma of hazelnut filled the small apartment. I sank into a chair. Think-ing of what Cliff and I would do once his plane landed and he could get to my apartment, I sipped my coffee. Then I noticed the blinking answering machine. My heart sank. If those Zwigs had started again . . .

I pressed the button for messages and was greeted with my mother's anxious voice. *"Simone! . . . Mama! I don't know if you've gotten home yet. No sooner than you had driven away, I got a call from Abe. Nat has been poisoned!"*

I slumped down in the chair and dialed Mama's number. "What happened?"

"Somebody poisoned the boy at the Melody Bar. That's where the ambulance picked him up."

"Where?" I repeated.

"The Melody Bar, near Monica!" Mama said.

I felt like a child who was being forced into something that didn't feel good. "Are you sure? Maybe he's not really—"

"Simone!" she snapped, in the special tone she uses when she knows I need to be pushed forward.

"Okay, okay," I said. "When did it happen?"

Mama's voice calmed slightly. "Last night," she answered, "or early this morning. I'm not sure!"

"What do you want me to do?" I asked, and cringed inwardly.

As I expected, Mama didn't hesitate. She loved investigating murders, and now she almost had another one to poke around into. "I need you to come home right away," she told me. "Today."

"Now? I just got home!"

"I want to go to that Melody Bar and talk to some of the people who were there; I can't go into a bar alone!"

Disbelief swept through me. "No," I said stubbornly. "I can't come today. You'll have to get Daddy to go with you. I can't come. No!"

"James has gone hunting, you know that."

I shook my head. "Then go by yourself," I said stubbornly.

"Simone, I don't feel comfortable going in there alone. It's not a nice place."

"Ask somebody else!"

"There is nobody else!"

"Then you'll just have to wait until next weekend, Mama!"

"Ask Cliff to drive you."

"Mama!" I yelled. "Cliff and I haven't seen each other in *weeks*. We need these few hours!"

"Simone, Hannah is dead, Nat may be dying, and—"

"Okay," I agreed, because experience had taught me this was an argument I couldn't win. "I'll talk to Cliff and call you back!" So much for a few precious hours with Cliff. I slammed the receiver down so hard I dropped the phone. After I'd rescued it, I sat on the couch, thumping a pillow with my fist. It's one of the ways I maturely deal with the unfairness of life.

Two hours and forty minutes later, I was looking back toward Atlanta as Cliff pulled my car onto the tree-lined I-20 and I headed east once more. He was in the driver's seat, wearing a pair of jeans, a sweatshirt, and a pair of brown suede Reebok walking shoes. When he glanced over at me and smiled, I knew why my heart ached to be alone with him.

"Tell me again," he asked, "why does Miss Candi insist that you come back to Otis today?"

"Remember I told you that Miss Hannah Mixon, our next-door neighbor's mother, died two weeks ago? Well, she was poisoned. Now her son Nat has been poisoned, too. Mama wants to go to the Melody Bar to talk to some of the people who were there when it happened."

Cliff adjusted the rearview mirror, then pulled smoothly into the inside lane. His speed picked up as we swiftly passed several cars on the right.

"The Melody Bar is a juke joint where Nat and his buddies hang out," I explained.

A car cut sharply in front of us. Cliff braked and swore under his breath. After the traffic had eased a little, he asked, "Why does your mother want to go to the bar today?"

"She thinks she might learn something."

"I know Miss Candi likes solving murders, but . . ." He shook his head.

"It's more to it than her solving the murders," I said.

Cliff's eyebrow rose.

"Miss Hannah willed land to Mama. And Mama thinks the land has something to do with the whole mess."

❦

Mama was in the foyer waiting for us. "I hated to call you back," she said, after hugging me and greeting Cliff warmly.

"Forget it," I said. After all, if finding out what might have happened to Nat was important to Mama, I guess it was important to me, too. "Did you find out anything more?"

"There's a lot of conflicting stories. But what I gathered so far is that the bar was very crowded last night and Nat was doing his usual drinking. Abe told me that the report is that Nat suddenly grabbed his throat, then fell to the floor. They got him to the hospital but he's hanging on by a thread!"

"What kind of poison was it?" I asked.

"The doctor isn't sure yet," Mama replied.

"Do you think the poisoner was somebody at the bar? One of Nat's friends?" I asked.

"Abe got a list of everybody who was there, and he's going to question each and every one." She reached for her jacket. "Right now, I want to go to the Melody Bar."

"Let's get this show on the road," Cliff said cheerfully. He grinned at me.

"Yeah," Mama said. "The sooner we get this over, the quicker you two can get back to Atlanta!"

❦

The Melody Bar is open seven nights a week. It's just as busy on Sunday night as any one of the others. The one big room was very dark, the smell of cigarette smoke mingled pungently with beer and Johnnie Red. Bursts of laughter punctuated the loud chatter; the jukebox pounded one continuous rap beat.

Cliff and I followed Mama through the smoky darkness toward a middle-aged man whose potbellied stomach hung over his old jeans. He wore a T-shirt that had once been white, and a pair of dirty running shoes. He was slouching in his chair, an empty beer glass and a full beer pitcher on the table. When he saw Mama, he bolted upright. "Miss Candi!" he exclaimed. "What you doing here?"

Mama motioned to him. "Relax, Buford," she said.

The man Mama had called Buford slouched down in his chair again. "I'm just having a little drink," he muttered as he poured beer from the pitcher.

Mama shook her head sadly as Cliff pulled a chair out for her. Buford tipped his glass and let the beer slide down his throat before speaking again. "This ain't no place for you, Miss Candi," he said.

"I agree that this isn't my usual hangout," Mama said pleasantly, "but I'm here trying to find out what happened to Nat Mixon."

Buford took a gulp of beer. "Nat got real sick last night. They took him to the hospital."

"Nat's maybe dying," I said.

Buford put his glass on the table. He squinted at me. "Something he ate?"

"The doctor says it's something he *drank*," Mama said.

Buford's eyes refused to meet Mama's. "We've all got to go sometime," he said.

"Somebody put something in Nat's drink last night," Mama told him.

"I don't know nothing about that. The place was full, just like now," Buford said.

Mama nodded. Somewhere behind us, a woman shrieked with laughter. "Was there anybody particular around Nat?" Mama asked Buford.

"Everybody. Nat had money last night, he was buying drinks for whoever walked into the door." Buford shrugged.

"Did he have an argument with anybody?" Cliff asked.

When Buford didn't answer, I placed my foot on top of Cliff's and applied a little pressure. This was my way of telling him that Buford wouldn't talk to him because he thought Cliff was a stranger. Cliff immediately understood. He sat back and surveyed the noisy room.

"Did he have an argument with anybody?" This time, Mama asked. Buford looked at Mama, then worked his tongue along his teeth, sucking, as if he were trying to clean them. "Nobody was bothering Nat, if that what you mean."

"Was there *anything* unusual?" Mama persisted. "Anything at all?"

Buford frowned. He slouched further into his chair. "Nothing that I saw," he said grimly.

Mama sighed, shook her head, and stood up. Cliff and I did, too.

"Do you remember," Mama asked as if it were an afterthought, "whether Nat mentioned that he smelled something funny, something that he had smelled before?"

Buford looked around, then chuckled sourly. "I don't know what he could have smelled funny in *here*!" he replied.

We followed Mama to the bar. There, she waved to a thick-lipped woman with stooped shoulders. The woman was light-skinned, but on one side of her face there was a liver spot the size of a half-dollar. Mama sat on a stool at the end of the bar until the woman walked over. Mama introduced her as Lulu, the owner of the Melody Bar.

"Death comes in threes," Lulu replied in a grim tone when Mama broached the subject of Nat's poisoning. "If Nat doesn't make it, some-body else will die before it stops!"

"Did Nat mention smelling something funny before he died?" Mama asked, not deterred by this expression of impending doom.

Lulu inhaled through her nose and waved Mama's question aside. "Ain't nothing wrong with my place," she muttered.

I was a little exasperated. "I don't know about that."

Lulu looked at me. Her eyes were eerily va-cant. "This your girl?" she asked Mama.

"This is my Simone," Mama replied. "And her good friend, Cliff."

Lulu stuck a Camel in the corner of her mouth. "Nat ain't mentioned nobody smelling funny to me!"

Mama frowned. "Was there anybody here other than the usual?"

"No." Lulu took a book of matches from her pocket and twirled it in her hand. "Nobody here but people who always be here." She struck a match and lit her cigarette.

"Could anybody have gotten to Nat's drink?" Mama asked. In the background, somebody dropped a glass and cursed when it shattered.

The record on the jukebox changed, although it didn't sound much different from the one that had been on. Lulu inhaled a lungful of blue smoke. She hesitated, as if she was thinking. "I don't know," she said finally, exhaling. "I've done told Abe all this. When the music is right and spirits are high, nobody pays any attention to nobody at the Melody!"

Mama took a deep breath as though she was trying to analyze what Lulu had just said. "Anybody you think I ought to talk to? Anybody who was particularly close to Nat?"

Lulu grinned. "You mean was he sleeping with any gal?"

Mama stared across the bar at her, saying nothing until Lulu blew another puff of smoke

111

and answered. "Nat bedded down with lots of girls. But two come to mind," she finally said.

"What's their names?" Mama asked.

Lulu glanced at me. "I don't remember seeing neither one of them was here last night."

"Their names?" Mama repeated firmly.

"I ain't for getting people in trouble who don't need no trouble, you know what I mean," Lulu said.

Mama nodded.

Lulu stared down at the bar counter, smeared a little spill of beer with her fingertip. Then she seemed to come to a decision. "This is between me and you. Nobody else got to know who Nat slept with off and on."

"I won't mention them to Abe," Mama promised.

Lulu nodded. You could see she believed Mama. People always do. "Nat mainly slept with Trudy Paige. From time to time he's slept with Portia Evans," she said.

Mama's eyebrow arched. "What do you know about these girls?" she asked.

Lulu's nostrils flared. "They do what they're big enough to do. Ain't no law against that!"

"Okay," Mama said. "I'll talk to them—"

Lulu looked anxious. "You won't get them in trouble?"

"No," Mama replied.

" 'Cuz, Candi, I can't swear either of those girls were here last night when Nat got sick."

Mama nodded thoughtfully. But I could tell she knew that Lulu lied.

CHAPTER
EIGHT

We were back outside gratefully filling our nostrils and lungs with cold fresh air.

Cliff had parked the Honda beside a large pine that was centered in a looped circular turnabout. I stood near the passenger's side waiting for my eyes to adjust after the gloomy, smoky darkness of the bar. I watched shadows, people going in and out of the club, in and out of the parking lot. My eyes were following one particular shadow when something on Mama's face caught my attention. "You okay?" I asked her, worried.

"I've made a big mistake," she murmured, so softly I wasn't sure I heard her.

The wind picked up; trees swayed. "What?"

"I should have known that whoever killed Hannah would try to kill Nat again. Especially after somebody hit him so brutally over his head."

I slipped my arm around her and hugged her. "The sheriff was supposed to be looking into that, not you," I reminded her. Cliff nodded, agreeing with me.

"It was what I was supposed to do!" she whispered back. I felt her body shiver. There was hurt in her dark eyes. I wanted to say something, something that would make a difference. But Mama was staring straight ahead, spooked by some worry or guilt I couldn't ease for her. Neither of us spoke. This was not my Mama, I thought. Not the self-styled detective who enjoys digging until she comes up with the truth. I suspected she was worried that the town's three gossiping women would learn of Miss Hannah's will before she could discover who had killed Miss Hannah and who had attacked Nat and then poisoned him. It was clear that my Mama wasn't relishing the search for the truth one bit.

The wind made a rushing sound through the dying leaves above us. "You can solve a murder, Mama, but there's no way you could have stopped what happened to Nat," I told her.

Mama's expression stayed serious, somber. She was trying to figure out something. "There must be . . ." she started, then shook her head. "That envelope . . ."

"What about the envelope?" I asked.

"I haven't found it!" Mama said. Her tone showed how frustrated she was.

Cliff cleared his throat. "You think the envelope will explain why somebody poisoned Nat?" he asked.

Mama made a gesture with her hand, like she was flicking away a fly. "Yes, I think that envelope may explain everything," she said softly. "We've got to go back into that house."

I stiffened. "Mama, you are not going to look for that envelope alone. Wait until Daddy comes home!"

Mama was about to reply when she seemed to notice something. She called out, "Moody, is that you?"

A tall, thin, hawk-faced man emerged from the trees. He silently stalked toward us. He reminded me of a human scarecrow.

Moody froze. He spread his hands, doing his best to look innocent, and failing. "Uh, what you doing out here, Miss Candi?" he said.

"Trying to get a fix on what happened to Nat last night," she told him, taking a few steps in his direction.

"What happened to Nat?" Moody demanded,

stepping back like Mama had just threatened his life.

Mama seemed to understand his skittishness: She didn't move any closer. "He's been poisoned right here at the bar."

Moody made a sound, but no words came from his thin lips. He just stood, his hands in his pockets, looking like my father does when he's trying to act cool.

"Can we talk?" Mama asked, gently.

Moody looked away, then pulled his collar up and the brim of his hat down. " 'Bout what?" he asked suspiciously.

"About Nat. About who would want to kill him," Mama replied.

Moody shook his head. He began shifting restlessly from one foot to the other. "I ain't got nothing to say about Nat's being poisoned," he mumbled.

"Did you talk to him last night? Maybe have a drink with him?" Mama asked.

Moody fumbled in his coat pocket like he was looking for something. "Naw," he said, after a long pause. "I ain't seen or talked to Nat for a couple of days."

"But you were here at the club last night when he got sick, weren't you?"

Again, Moody was slow to speak. For a moment I thought he wasn't going to answer

Mama. He wiped his nose with his hand. Then he turned and walked toward the door of the bar. His thin body moved like fluid, like smoke. "I ain't got to answer no questions from you," he tossed over his shoulder.

"That's not like Moody," Mama said, to Cliff and me. "Not like him at all! His grandma raised him better than that."

Moody stopped. He turned back to face us. "I ain't had nothing to do with what happened to Nat!" he insisted. But his voice was a bit shaky now. Then he scurried inside the bar.

Mama watched after him with concern. "Something is wrong with that boy," she told us. "I'll have to get James to check him out."

"I don't think he liked Nat," I said.

"Moody is a good boy," Mama said.

"Good people become killers," I pointed out. "Isn't he the same man we saw outside Nat's front door the other night, the one who decided *not* to go inside?"

Mama's face lit up. "Simone, you're right. That's exactly who we saw!"

"Mama, I would be real interested to hear Moody's explanation of what he was doing at Nat's house that night, but not right now. I've been ignoring my bladder too long; I've got to go to the bathroom."

"Can you wait until we get back to the house?" Cliff asked.

"No, it can't wait," I said curtly. When in distress, I'm always extremely honest.

Mama pointed. "I saw a sign in the back, near the phone."

"Come with me. I don't like walking through that place alone."

Mama smiled, then she nodded.

Cliff checked his watch; car keys jingled in his hand. "Hurry up, it's getting late, Simone. I'll warm up the car."

Mama and I pushed our way to the rear of the bar into a small musty hall lined with boxes and broken furniture. Bathrooms and a telephone were at its end. My bladder was so full it felt like it was going to burst. I hit the door to the ladies' room with my shoulder like a quarterback. I slipped into a narrow stall, snapped the latch, then danced through pulling down jeans, tights, and panties.

When I flushed the toilet, piled back on my clothes, and reopened the stall door, I found Mama talking to a young woman in her mid-twenties.

"Simone," Mama said. "This is Pauline Singleton. Pauline's mother and I work together."

The young woman turned to me. She was large-framed with a chubby face, a mouth full of gold teeth, and enough weave in her head to stuff a good-sized pillow. All of her clothes were bright purple. I said hello and smiled at her.

"Were you here in the club last night?" Mama asked Pauline.

Pauline began to brush her voluminous hair. "Yeah, me and about fifty other people. Why?"

"Did you see Nat Mixon?"

Pauline nodded.

"How was he?" Mama asked.

"He was doing good, setting everybody up, buying everybody liquor."

"Did you see anybody near him?" Mama persisted.

Pauline, who was now fishing in her purse, hesitated, staring down at her lipstick, which was a bright orange color. Then she shrugged. "Everybody was near him. I told you, he was *buying!*"

"Did you hear or see anything funny?" Mama asked. I knew her well enough to know how impatient she was becoming.

Pauline dropped her lipstick back into her purse, brushed her hair back behind her ears. She was silent, as if trying to think of something to say, then she shook her head.

"Did you *smell* something funny?"

Pauline pulled out a small change purse and headed for the door. She made an impatient gesture with her hand. "I've got to go," she said. "Got to call to check on my kids!" Mama followed. I could see that she was hot on the trail of some clue, searching for something.

When I finished washing my hands, I joined them. They stood next to the pay telephone in the crowded hall. Pauline had the phone off the hook but she was looking Mama straight in her eyes. "Did Nat say anything to you?" Mama was saying.

Pauline dropped the phone in its cradle. Mama's face tightened but Pauline gazed placidly back. "You got a quarter?" she asked Mama.

Mama pulled out her wallet. "No," she said. "Simone?"

I fished in my pockets, then glanced back at Mama. "No," I said.

Pauline wrinkled her nose, inhaled through it and announced, "I've got to get change." She walked past us in the direction of the bar. I hadn't realized till then how powerful her perfume was. I sneezed.

Mama began massaging her temples. Her eyes were glued to Pauline's swaying hips.

"Why are you pushing her so hard?" I asked.

Mama pulled a piece of paper and a pencil from her pocketbook, looked at the phone dial, then scribbled down the telephone number. She sighed. "That girl is hiding something!"

"What makes you so sure?"

"I *know*," Mama snapped.

"She looks like she's got it together to me."

"Pauline is loose, free-spirited. She's holding herself tight 'cause she doesn't want to tell me something!"

When Pauline returned, I tried taking a closer look, trying to be Mama, to sense what the girl must be hiding. But, unlike Mama, I must have been too obvious, because Pauline glared open-eyed directly back at me. "You see something that's bothering you?" she asked.

"I'm cool," I said, stepping back. Mama gave her head a little shake at me.

Pauline dialed a number and spoke. After a few sentences, she put the phone back on its hook and turned to Mama. "I've told you everything I know," she said, sullenly. "Nat was buying the liquid, everybody was drinking it until somebody slipped him a mickey. That's all I know. Nothing else!"

Mama took a deep breath, then let it out. "I need to know if Nat said anything." She sounded absolutely determined to make Pauline reveal something that would help her in her investigation.

Pauline shut her dark eyes for a moment. Then opened them and snapped her fingers. "Yeah," she said in a tone that signaled she had decided to say what was on her mind whether Mama liked it or not. "Nat did tell me something before he blacked out. When he fell to the floor, I was the nearest person to him. I got down on my knees, you know, trying to see what I could do."

"Of course," Mama said, encouraging her.

A mocking smirk flickered at the corners of Pauline's wide mouth.

"Did Nat say something to you?" Mama repeated. I had never seen Mama more intent.

"Yeah," the girl replied. "I wasn't going to tell anybody about it 'cause I didn't know how much truth there was to it."

"Go on," Mama insisted.

Knowing how badly Mama wanted to clear up Miss Hannah's death and the attempts on Nat's life before anybody learned about the contents of Miss Hannah's will, I can only imagine what she felt when Pauline said, "Nat whispered that you'd talked his Mama into giving you his two hundred and fifty acres. He said you were trying to kill him to keep from giving that land back to him!"

CHAPTER
NINE

It was two weeks before I would get back to Otis, although Mama and I talked nightly on the phone.

Several things happened during that time: Nat Mixon died forty-eight hours after he'd been poisoned. The doctors were surprised, Mama reported. At one point it looked like Nat was going to pull through. But he never came out of the coma.

Fortunately, it would appear that Pauline Singleton hadn't repeated Nat's dying words to anyone but Mama and me. As soon as she had a chance, Mama talked to Sarah Jenkins, Annie Mae Gregory, and Carrie Smalls, but they didn't once mention the Mixon land. Mama was sure that their neglect could only mean that they didn't know about it. Still, she felt time was running out. It was only a matter of weeks before Hannah's will would become public knowledge through the Probate Court.

Mama attended Nat's funeral. She told me she got a chance to see both of Nat's girlfriends, too. She visited Portia Evans at her home on Palmetto Street later that week. Portia told Mama that the night Nat was poisoned she'd been in Savannah. The man who was in the house with her when Mama visited confirmed Portia's story; they'd been together, he insisted.

Mama visited Trudy Paige's apartment twice but could never find her at home. She did speak to Trudy on the telephone, however, and got her to agree to meet at the Country Café on Ray Street. Trudy never showed. Mama asked me to run a paper check on Trudy. I contacted the Motor Vehicle Bureau and pulled her driver's license. From there I got her Social Security number and then her credit report. Trudy's last place of employment was listed as Otis General Hospital. She was a nurses' aide, something that was interesting since Nat had died at Otis General Hospital.

Mama called Daddy's cousin, Gertrude, who was a nurse at Otis General. Gertrude told Mama that Trudy had worked at the hospital but, after Nat died, she'd quit her job there. Gertrude said Trudy had told her she was leaving the area, moving up North to live with her sister.

Next, Mama called on Sheriff Abe to locate Trudy. He promised to do whatever he could. But Abe made it clear he had no legal cause to look for the girl; nothing gave him reason to suspect that she had broken the law.

The envelope that Miss Hannah had mentioned to Calvin Stokes when she'd made up her will still hadn't surfaced. The missing Bible showed up, however—back in Nat's house. The map and photograph were still inside it, Mama told me. I suggested to her that it was Nat who had been hiding in the shadows the night Mama, Daddy, and I visited his house. Later, he'd seen us hurry away to the hospital to check on Uncle Chester. Mama admitted that neither she nor my father could remember whether or not they had set the security alarm that night. We agreed that Nat had simply slipped into our house and had taken back what was rightfully his.

Mama told me that she had asked Daddy to take the map and picture over to Uncle Chester. She wanted to know whether or not Uncle Chester, one of the oldest residents of the county, could identify the house in the photograph. It was a long shot, but . . .

It was nearly six o'clock Friday evening when I grabbed my coat and my shoulder bag. I walked two blocks to the side street where I'd parked my car. The air was cold and fresh; winter was certainly here. I drove over to Peachtree and Fourteenth Street in Buckhead to the Italian restaurant where I was to meet Cliff for dinner. When I walked in, he stood immediately and kissed me, his lips icy cold from his drink. "You like this restaurant?" he asked.

I put my handbag on the floor and eased onto the seat across from him. "I like *you*," I told him.

Cliff held his hand up for the waiter, who moved over to the table and poured me a glass of Chardonnay, then put a Caesar salad in front of me. The little restaurant was more authentic than elegant, with red-and-white-checked table-cloths, voices calling from the kitchen, the scent of garlic filling the air and stimulating the appetite. We were the only customers; at a nearby table three waiters sat eating their dinner before the rush.

Cliff held up his wineglass and I held up mine, tapping my glass against his with a *ting*. "To us," he said.

"Forever," I said.

When Cliff smiled, I felt a pleasurable stirring.

He ordered for both of us: veal cooked in white wine, and linguini in a marinara sauce with clams and mussels. When it came, I leaned close to my plate and inhaled. The rich aroma was worth the wait.

By now, the restaurant had filled with people. Dishes rattled, the voices of other diners filled the air. I sipped from my glass, smiled, and ate everything on my plate, then I sighed happily. I'd completely forgotten the two murders in Otis.

When we left the restaurant, the wind gusts carried cold and moisture from the mountains. Cliff took my hand and led me to his car in the parking lot. "What about my Honda?" I asked.

"We'll pick it up in the morning," he said.

"It's going to snow tonight," I whispered.

"Let it," Cliff said. "You and I don't have any place to go!"

When we got to my apartment, Cliff swept me up in his arms and carried me through the front door and straight to the couch.

Despite the coldness of the night, the wine had warmed me. Cliff's breath tickled my ear and I started laughing. His arms tightened around me, pulling me closer; I felt locked in a tight cocoon, safe and protected. Murder seemed very far away.

Through the fabric of my dress, I felt his large

hands on my back, warm, strong, pressing me into him. I caught a hint of his scent, and when he kissed me, I tasted wine.

The phone rang. I jumped in Cliff's arms. Instinctively, I opened my eyes and reached for the receiver.

Cliff's embrace didn't loosen. "Don't answer it," he murmured.

"It could be an emergency," I protested.

"So what?" he said carelessly.

Again I reached for the receiver, but when Cliff touched my hand, I stopped. Three more rings and the answering machine picked up. My father's frightened voice filled the room.

"Simone, for God's sake, if you're there, pick up the phone!"

I squirmed away from Cliff, ignoring his scowl, and snatched up the receiver. "Calm down, Daddy. What's the matter?" As I listened, my stomach began hurting, a pain that moved from the top to the bottom like somebody had a knife in my gut. "Okay, we'll be there as soon as we can," I said, then gently put the phone back onto its receiver. My hands were icy cold and trembling.

Cliff gave me a direct look, his brown eyes soft, gentle. "What's wrong? Simone, what's happened?"

"Mama has been poisoned," I whispered, unable to believe my own words.

Cliff's eyebrow arched, his mouth opened.

"She's in Otis General Hospital fighting for her life," I told him.

CHAPTER
TEN

This drive to Otis was eerie. Like some kind of twisted nightmare. At times I had the feeling Cliff's car was standing still, with the lights zooming by as we stayed motionless in the road. We hit Interstate 20, heading east toward Augusta. The wind hissed across the highway. I shivered and hunched my shoulders, trying to work things through my mind.

We must have passed twenty ten-wheelers, but the big trucks stayed to the right and none followed us when we pulled off onto 125, the highway that took us through the Savannah River Plant. I watched the sky. The clouds whipped overhead like black ships. The full moon slid between them, disappearing, then peeking out again. I shivered.

"Why would anybody want to kill Mama?" I asked Cliff.

"We'll find out," he said.

"I keep seeing it in my mind," I said. "Mama doubling over in pain."

He was silent as I spoke, watching me. "Miss Candi is a strong woman. She'll be all right."

Neither of us talked after that. A wintry gust nudged the little car, and I wondered what my father would do if Mama died. The thought made me shudder. I was scared. I folded my arms against my chest and stared out the window.

We finally reached Boldercrest. I glanced at my watch. One A.M. Why poison Mama? This whole business had turned crazy. It had to be that Mixon land, that cursed soil that someone thought more of than life or death. Why hadn't she gotten rid of it, I thought in despair. "Whatever Calvin had to do to influence Judge Thompson, he'd do it," I said, not realizing I'd spoken aloud.

"What?" Cliff asked, confused.

My thoughts were moving like a freight train. "No amount of dirt is worth my Mama's life."

Cliff touched my arm. "You're right," he said.

When Cliff and I finally reached the hospital,

he dropped me off at the front entrance. I ran inside to find my father. He was in the intensive care unit, standing in the hall like a lost child.

I took a deep breath to steady myself. The smell of antiseptic stung my nostrils. As I walked toward him, I thought that he looked older, wearier; my heart twisted at the thought that for once he was having to take care of Mama. "Is she going to be okay?" I asked, hugging him.

"I don't know," he said hoarsely. I wondered if he'd been crying.

It's difficult for me to say exactly the way I felt now, having to face the possibility of Mama dying. I remembered how she and I talked earlier, remembered how she told me that there was no way to prepare for death. My world had never felt so vulnerable. So scary.

A doctor came over to speak to us. He said his name was DeFoe. He led us to some chairs near a window and asked us to sit down. "We've done all that we can do," he told us. Cliff, who had joined us, took my hand. He held it tight.

"Is she going to be all right?" Daddy asked.

"You're her husband?" the doctor asked.

Daddy nodded.

The doctor was a dumpy-looking man, soft and pale and too heavy, going bald, short of breath. He looked out of tired brown eyes, showing no reaction at all to our pain. "It appears that your wife has been poisoned," he said.

Daddy nodded.

"The sheriff will want to talk with you."

Daddy took a deep breath. "I'll talk to Abe later," he told the doctor. "Right now I want to know about Candi. Will she be okay?"

Dr. DeFoe didn't answer his question. "From her symptoms, we suspect she ingested poison, some form of arsenic, but we won't be certain until after we get lab results. We've pumped her stomach. We're sending her stomach contents to the state lab in Columbia. They'll tell us exactly what the poison was."

Daddy's hand trembled; beads of sweat were on his forehead. "Will Candi be okay?" he repeated.

"She's in a coma. We'll know more tomorrow," the doctor said wearily, then got up and plodded away, his shoulders hunched against the unending misery of his chosen profession.

Daddy watched the doctor go out of sight. "That's what I hate about hospitals, doctors. They don't know nothing and they don't tell you anything."

Cliff put his arm around my shoulders and together we followed my father down a corridor. Doctors, nurses, and orderlies walked past. No one seemed to notice us.

We found a soft drink machine. Standing at the machine with his back to us, Daddy pulled wildly at the levers. "I can't get this damn thing to work," he muttered.

"I'll do it," Cliff said, taking the dollar from Daddy's hand and turning George Washington's face the proper way. "Diet Coke?" he asked.

Daddy reached into his inside coat pocket and fished out a pack of chewing gum. "I don't drink or eat anything diet," he said.

I couldn't bear to wait any longer. "Tell me what happened."

Daddy cleared his throat. His eyes were bleary. "Simone, honey, I'm not sure of what happened. This is what I do know. Around five o'clock Candi called me from her office. She told me she had to stop by the hospital before she could get home for supper. Somebody had reported that a child had been taken to the hospital. The child had signs of abuse."

I glanced up and down the hallway. Being here like this made me feel strange, nauseated and dizzy as if I hadn't eaten all day.

"Go on, Mr. James," Cliff encouraged.

"Candi is the Case Manager who's on twenty-four-hour duty this week, so she was the one who had to investigate." Daddy faltered.

My skin tightened. I searched Daddy's face for something that made sense of what had happened.

Daddy shifted his weight from one foot to the other. "When Candi got here at the hospital, there was confusion. Nobody knew anything about an abused child. Candi telephoned me again. She told me to put the baked beans with beef casserole into the oven because she was coming home. Simone, that was the last time I spoke to your mother." He hesitated. "The rest is what I got from Gertrude. She talked to the people here at the hospital for me."

He continued. "Martha Furman, the admission clerk, told Gertrude that Candi came in around five-fifteen saying that the agency had gotten a report that an abused child had been brought into the hospital. Martha made a few phone calls but she couldn't find anybody who knew anything about the child. Martha told Candi that there was no report of an incident. Your mother seemed satisfied. Martha saw Candi leave the hospital. An hour later, Candi returned. She told Martha that she was convinced that an abused child was in the hospital and that she wasn't going to leave until she found the child."

"Sounds like my determined mother," I said.

Daddy nodded. "Bowie Thomas, an orderly,

told Gertrude that he saw Candi in the hospital parking lot around five-thirty. He remembers because he'd gone out there for a cigarette break. Bowie told Gertrude that Candi was talking to a woman."

My heart quickened. "What woman?" I asked.

"Bowie said he didn't recognize the woman. She was wearing a coat, and had on a hat. He does remember that she had on white shoes, so he thought maybe she worked here at the hospital."

Daddy took another shuddery breath. He pointed toward the corridor that led to the Emergency Room. "Gertrude says that Velma Pickens, the Emergency Room nurse, remembers that Candi came into the ER around six-twenty asking about an abused child."

"So, in the hour that Mama first arrived, she talked to Martha, left the hospital, where Bowie saw her talking to the woman in the parking lot, returned to talk to Martha again and finally ended up in the Emergency Room talking to Velma. Is that right?" I asked.

Daddy nodded. "As far as I know, that is what happened."

"Did anybody see Mama leave the hospital a second time?"

Daddy looked down at the untouched soda can in his hand. "No. Martha told Gertrude she didn't see Candi leave again, but she did say she felt that Candi had finally given up her search for the child and had gone home. She said she was surprised when she learned that Candi was in the Emergency Room complaining of dizziness and pains in her stomach."

I patted Daddy's arm. "We'll find out what happened, and we'll find the person who—"

"Why would anybody try to kill Miss Candi in a hospital, where she could get medical attention immediately?" Cliff asked. His tone was urgent.

"That's a good question." The deep frown between Daddy's eyebrows gave him the appearance of being older than he was. "But when I get my hands on the s.o.b. who did this to Candi, I'll—" He turned away.

"Take it easy," I whispered, hoping to calm both of us. I thought about my brothers; they would have to be told. "Did you call Will and Rodney?"

Daddy was silent and I could see that he was scared stiff of the thought of Mama's dying. Not calling my brothers meant not having to acknowledge how ill she was. "I'll call them tomorrow." He said it curtly.

"How much of what happened are you going to tell them?"

I looked at Cliff; his question surprised me. Why wouldn't we tell my brothers everything?

"If my guess is right, Will and Rodney are going to want to know who poisoned Miss Candi, who hated her enough to want her dead," Cliff went on. "For them to understand what has happened here, you're going to have to tell them about Miss Hannah's and Nat's deaths."

For an instant, I felt funny, like somebody was staring at me from a distance. Would whoever had murdered the Mixons add my Mama to his list of victims?

Daddy's skin was gray. "The doctor said he thought she'd been given arsenic. Abe told Candi that the lab reports showed that both Nat and Miss Hannah were poisoned with arsenic," he said.

I tried to say something to him, then crossed my arms in front of me, trying to control what felt like a tumor blossoming in my chest, pushing my lungs and taking up the space they needed to breathe so that I had to gasp out loud to fill them with air. When I couldn't hold on any longer, I started to cry, feeling oddly uncomforted by my father's trembling embrace.

CHAPTER
ELEVEN

Nights and days inside hospitals are too much alike. The hours blurred. Saturday morning. Saturday night. There was no change in Mama's condition. She remained in a coma.

Sarah Jenkins, Annie Mae Gregory, and Carrie Smalls visited, stopping by the room. I tried not to show my resentment. Their display of concern was only a ploy to be the first to get information about Mama's condition. Fortunately, other friends from Otis came by, too. Daddy wouldn't talk to them. It was my job to keep them from gawking at Mama like she was some sort of sleeping beauty. Sheriff Abe visited, too. He stood for a long time, looking down at

Mama. Then he promised Daddy he would find out whoever had done this to Mama and left.

Mama's room was large and sunny, a long rectangle that had another bed in it. The second bed was unoccupied. My father used the other bed whenever he felt the need, but the truth is he didn't sleep much.

Neither did I. I pulled a chair close beside Mama and took her hand in mine; it felt soft and warm, as if nothing were really wrong with her. But her forehead was damp with sweat, her breathing rasped. This whole evil thing felt like an illusion, a deceitful maze of events that must have a way out. Who'd try to murder Mama? A serial killer? In Otis? It didn't seem possible. Some psychopath who got a kick out of poisoning innocent people? What could be behind Miss Hannah's and Nat's deaths? Was Mama, even unconscious, still in terrible danger? Suddenly it hit me. The thought came like a thunderbolt. Could Miss Hannah have known that somebody would kill for her land? Is that why she had entrusted it to Mama?

Daddy slept restlessly in the other bed. A nurse came into the room. She had a fifty-year-old face and a twenty-five-year-old body. Her uniform seemed perfumed with the sour smell of antiseptic. She nodded at me, but said nothing.

Silent, she walked around Mama's bed and

checked the electronic gadgets that monitored Mama's vital signs. Then she made a few notes and left the room. I moved closer to my mother, holding her hand tightly in mine. *Please get well, Mama*, I prayed. *Please.*

Cliff came into the room, and for a while watched me watch Mama. Then, he asked me to come outside with him. I didn't want to leave Mama but he reminded me that with my father asleep in the next bed, the odds of anybody doing anything to Mama were remote. Still, I didn't want to leave. Finally, Cliff coaxed me by insisting that I needed a break and some food. I squeezed Mama's hand and whispered my promise to be back soon.

Five minutes later, we sat in the lobby. Cliff had bought us coffee.

"When I telephoned Sidney," Cliff said, reminding me that it was he who had called my boss and told him of Mama's situation, "I got the impression that he wanted to speak to you directly."

"Sidney called me," I said. "I spoke to him yesterday. I couldn't tell him any more than you could. I promised him that if Mama makes any change, I'd call him again." I sipped my coffee and watched Cliff eat. The coffee was dreadful. "Nat said something," I recalled.

"What?" he asked.

"Nat said the person who hit him over the head had a funny smell."

Cliff's eyebrow rose. "Did he say what kind of a smell?"

"No. What made me think about it was that nurse who came into Mama's room a few minutes ago."

"Why?"

"Nurses . . . Doctors . . . Hospital workers smell funny, don't you think?"

Cliff frowned.

"It's the soap they wash with so many times a day. After a while, they smell like it's coming from their pores," I said.

"You think somebody from the *hospital* attacked Nat?"

"And maybe poisoned his mother, poisoned him and—" I stopped short.

"There are other smells that I would consider funny other than the soap that hospital workers use to scrub themselves," Cliff objected.

"My cousin Gertrude told Daddy that the woman that orderly saw talking to Mama in the parking lot might have been a hospital worker. Remember, she had on white shoes? The lab report confirmed that arsenic poisoned Mama. A hospital worker could easily get arsenic, don't you think?"

"Simone," Cliff said. "I know you're upset but

you've got to approach this thing with logic. First of all, even if it was arsenic Miss Candi ingested, we don't know how she got the poison."

"Okay," I said. "But if Mama was given arsenic, the same kind of poison that killed Miss Hannah and Nat. A hospital worker could have easily given it to all three of them, don't you think?"

"Working in a hospital makes certain poisons easily accessible, yes," Cliff agreed. "And I remember reading that during the 1800s and 1900s doctors used arsenic to treat syphilis, but I doubt they use it anymore. Arsenic's probably too old-fashioned to use as a medicine these days."

"I'll ask Gertrude," I said.

Cliff must have noted the chill in my tone. He touched my hand. "Simone, it didn't have to come from a hospital. You can get arsenic from other places easily," he pointed out.

"What other places?" I asked, unconvinced.

"A hardware store," he said. "People still use it to kill rats."

I shuddered, then drank the last sip of coffee. It tasted distinctly different from the ones Mama perked. Tears stung my eyes.

Mama opened her eyes at exactly six o'clock Sunday morning, thirty-six hours after she'd mysteriously slipped into a coma. Cliff and I had just talked my father into going home. We were expecting my two brothers to arrive any minute. Daddy needed a shave, and a change of clothes. When he balked, Cliff volunteered to drive him to the house and promised Daddy that he'd make me do the same thing later that afternoon. I kissed them both good-bye and once again took the chair close to Mama's bed.

For the first time since I had arrived, I was alone at Mama's side. I closed my eyes and prayed. "James," a voice whispered, so softly that I almost couldn't hear it. "James . . ." I rushed into the lobby in time to catch Daddy and Cliff before they had gotten out of the door. "Daddy, she's asking for you!" I cried.

Seconds later, Daddy was at Mama's side. "Candi," he whispered in a voice I'd never heard before. "You're going to be all right, baby, you're going to be all right!"

"I know," Mama whispered. Her voice was weak but confident.

"We're here," Daddy continued. "Me and Simone are here for you."

Mama nodded.

"Will and Rodney will be here soon," he whispered.

145

Mama's hand moved a little against the sheets. "They don't have—"

"Hush," Daddy whispered in a tender voice. "We're here for you, baby. Just like you've always been here for us!"

Mama smiled. Then she closed her eyes.

Daddy's cousin walked into the room. Gertrude wasn't dressed in her hospital uniform. She wore a pair of black slacks, a bulky black sweater, and shiny black boots. I wiped the tears from my face and motioned her to follow me out into the hall. "Do you use arsenic in this hospital?" I asked, once we were outside the room.

Gertrude shook her head. "No," she said. "Why do you ask?"

Cliff, who had followed us, eyed me.

"I thought maybe the person who poisoned Mama got the stuff from the hospital," I said.

"Simone," Cliff interjected sternly, "it's possible that your mother was poisoned somewhere else."

"It's ridiculous to think that somebody who works here would want to hurt Candi." Gertrude sounded angry. "I know practically everybody here—Ain't nobody got a grudge against Candi!"

"Could you get me a list of the names of everybody who works at the hospital?"

Gertrude seemed personally offended by my request. "For God's sake, why?"

"Just get me the list," I insisted.

Gertrude's eyebrows rose. "It'll take a while," she grumbled reluctantly. "But you're wrong, Simone. Nobody at this hospital has a grudge against Candi."

❦

Around noon my brothers arrived. Will, the younger, is a tall muscular man. Raised by a military father who made him develop his body, Will envisioned himself like my father. But after a short stint in the military, he got a job driving a UPS truck. He lives in Orlando, and has worked at the same place for the past ten years.

Rodney, my older brother, on the other hand, hated discipline, hated the military, hated predictability. He's tall, lean, and smooth. What physical acrobatics Will performed, Rodney performed academically. He finished college tops in his class, then set out immediately to New York where he landed a job in advertising sales for a national magazine. I'd never been more glad to see my brothers.

❦

Mama was weak but, with her family gathered around her sickbed, she insisted on telling us how she got poisoned. "Things started going wrong an hour after I arrived at the office," she said. "First somebody tried to break into my car."

Daddy was surprised. "You didn't tell me that when you called," he said.

Mama pushed herself up on her pillow. "Whoever it was didn't get inside, but the car alarm got stuck and it took an hour before I finally got it turned off. Around noon, I decided to go get lunch. When I got to my car it had two flat tires—I only had one spare."

Daddy was anxious now. "Those tires are practically new ones. There's no reason for them to be flat."

"Well, they were," Mama said.

"Where are the tires now?" Daddy asked.

"Jake, at the Exxon, towed the car to his station on Elm Street. I bought two new tires and had them put on the car. I guess Jake has the old ones," Mama said.

"I want to get those tires to see if they were defective," Daddy said.

"Good idea," Will agreed. "You might be able to get some money back from the company that sold them to you."

"Anyway," Mama continued, "because of the flat tires, I never did get lunch. Five o'clock, when I was about to walk out of the door, I got a phone call from the hospital."

"That's when you first called me?" Daddy asked.

Mama nodded. "I was so tired and hungry but I felt I had no choice, I had to go. After all, there was a hurt child here who needed my help."

"Martha Furman said you talked to her."

"Yeah," Mama said. "When no one knew anything about the child, Martha called the hospital's social worker, who told her that there was no report of an abused child. That's when I called you again, James."

"And the woman in the parking lot?" I asked.

Mama seemed stunned. "How did you know that?" she asked.

"An orderly told us," Cliff said.

"Did you know the woman?" I asked. "The woman in the parking lot?"

"Yes," Mama replied. "It was Trudy Paige, Nat's girlfriend. I'd been trying to get to talk to her and there she was, standing beside my car."

"What did she say to you?" Cliff asked.

"For one thing, she told me that she hadn't quit her job here at the hospital. And she told me that she had seen a child who showed signs of abuse in the hospital less than an hour earlier."

"Go on," I urged her.

"Trudy told me that the little boy belonged to one of the doctors. That the doctor's wife was an alcoholic and that during her binges she put matches to the child's body. She said that she thought that the reason nobody wanted to tell me about the boy was because they liked the doctor. They didn't want to cause him any trouble."

"And you fell for that?" I exclaimed. My voice was a bit louder than I wanted it to be. Mama frowned at me.

"I'm sorry," I apologized quickly. "Go on with your story."

"At the time, I was interested in talking to Trudy about Nat. I suggested to her that we go to get something to eat. I told her I had skipped lunch and that I needed a cup of coffee and a sandwich to pull me through. Trudy agreed. I got into my car, she got into hers and promised to meet me at the Country Café. When I got to the café, I ordered a hamburger and coffee and waited. When the waitress set my food in front of me, Trudy still hadn't arrived. My first thought was to go home to my own supper. After all, the hospital staff was probably right. Maybe somebody was playing a prank on me and there was no abused child. I was about to leave when the waitress came over and said I had a phone call. The woman on the phone told me that she was calling for Trudy because she had gotten held up at the hospital. She said Trudy wanted me to wait for her, she was on her way."

"And you waited?" I asked.

"I went back to the table, drank my coffee, and ate that hamburger," Mama said. "Trudy still didn't show."

"So why did you go back to the hospital?" Daddy demanded.

"I got another phone call. This time, the same woman told me that the child had been located and that I was needed at the hospital right away. She sounded panicky, very convincing. I went back to the hospital, talked to Martha again. Then I headed for the Emergency Room, thinking the child might be there and Martha hadn't gotten word about it yet. I hadn't been there but a few minutes when I started feeling dizzy."

"We know the rest." Daddy's face showed signs of the battle he'd just gone through trying to deal with the possibility of Mama's death.

The words weren't out of his mouth when Cousin Agatha wheeled Uncle Chester into the room. Uncle Chester himself had been discharged from the hospital a couple of weeks earlier. He was in a wheelchair now, his bony frame tucked under mounds of blankets, a huggy cap pulled down to his shiny eyes.

"Uncle Chester, you didn't have to come to see me," Mama said, startled that the old man

would allow Agatha to take him out of his be-
loved house. He hated the hospital.

Uncle Chester's eyes burned. "I know I didn't
have to come," he snapped. "Don't have to do
anything I don't want to do!"

Mama smiled. "Well, I'm glad to see you, glad
you thought enough of me to visit."

"Agatha tried to stop me, but she knows better than to hinder me from what I want to do,"
growled the old man. "Listen, Candi, I come
here to tell you, just like I told Agatha, you best
be careful whose pot you dip into from now on. I
don't expect to be eating from many of the pots
that get sent to my house anymore myself." He
said it very firmly, like all of Otis was out to get
him.

Cliff, my father and brothers laughed, but I
knew better than to give Uncle Chester cause
for scolding me. "What's ailing you all?" he
snapped, his eyes coldly staring at my father.
"James boy, I done told you, God don't bless you
when you laugh at old people."

"I'm sorry, Uncle Chester," Daddy said.

"I ain't looking for sorry. Don't do it again!"

"Yes, sir," Daddy said, respectfully.

Mama decided to come to Daddy's rescue.
"Uncle Chester," she said, "did you recognize
the place in the picture I sent to you?" she
asked.

"Candi, what are you talking about?" Uncle Chester growled.

"I sent a piece of paper with a drawing of a barn and maybe a shed to you by James. Attached to it was a picture of an old house, remember?"

Uncle Chester looked puzzled.

Cousin Agatha put her hand over her mouth and spoke down toward her father's right ear. "You and I talked about the picture," she reminded her father. "You said it was the Gordon place."

Uncle Chester made a short sound that I assume was a snort of recognition. "When I was a young man, a woman named Stella Gordon was born and raised at that place," he said. He snorted again. Then he coughed.

"Stella was an only child," he continued. "Her Mama and Daddy died of the Spanish flu back in '18. They owned two hundred and fifty acres of land. The Gordons left all that land to Stella."

Mama shifted in her bed, but she did not interrupt Uncle Chester.

"The man who married Stella was named Mixon," Uncle Chester told us. "Leroy Mixon. He farmed Stella's land and he did pretty good with it, too. But Leroy was mean and he didn't love Stella or their only child, a real sickly boy named Reeves."

When Uncle Chester stopped to catch his breath, nobody spoke. But I could see that Mama's eyes were bright with curiosity.

Finally, he started talking again. "When Reeves was about ten, talk was that Leroy came home from the fields and started beating up on Stella. He hit her so hard she fell and hit her head on the corner of the table. Stella died; Leroy buried her in the Cypress Creek Cemetery. A week after he buried Stella, Leroy married a widow, a woman who had a son."

"Hannah Mixon?" I asked.

"I reckon," Uncle Chester said. "My eyes ain't much what it use to be, but I'll swear that picture is of Stella Gordon's house."

"Hannah Mixon, Leroy Mixon," Mama murmured, as if talking to herself.

"Mind you, Candi, that land got blood on it," Uncle Chester declared sourly. "Tainted land ain't good for nothing, not even burying. Do you know that when Leroy died, he didn't even leave the land to his own boy, he and Stella's son. Good-for-nothing Leroy left the whole thing to Hannah Mixon and her boy."

It was ill-timed but when I realized it, it was too late—I had already spoken. "That's why it makes sense to form the Covington Land Company and incorporate it."

"Ain't no law going to take over the Covington land!" Uncle Chester squawked. His beady eyes bulged. "I done told Agatha, and I—"

"Uncle Chester," Mama interrupted smoothly. "Simone's right. At least hear me out before you close your mind."

"My mind ain't never been closed. I ain't signing no papers," he muttered.

"Do you want the Covington land to end up like Leroy Mixon's land?" she asked. "Do you want people that ain't no kin to the Covingtons to get our land?"

"Ain't nobody but Covingtons are going to profit from that land." Uncle Chester said it fiercely.

Cousin Agatha spoke up. "When you're dead and gone," she told her father, "you won't have nothing to say about the Covington land. Now, while you're alive and able, you need to make provision for it."

Uncle Chester didn't say anything for a full minute. We were all smart enough to stay silent. Then he said, "I'm tired. Candi, when you get back home, fix me some of your lamb stew and don't let nobody get near the pot until you get it to me." He cut his eyes toward Agatha. "Take me home," he ordered. "My bed is calling for me."

After Uncle Chester and Cousin Agatha had gone, Mama closed her eyes. I was about to suggest that we all go out into the lobby while Mama rested, when Sarah Jenkins, Annie Mae Gregory, and Carrie Smalls sashayed into the room. The women clustered beside Mama's bed, looking on with pitying eyes. "I declare," Annie Mae Gregory said, "I never thought there was so much spitefulness in this town."

Mama opened her eyes and rested them on the women's faces. "I didn't hear you come in," she said.

Annie Mae Gregory must have thought what she had said was worth repeating because she said it again. "I never thought there was so much spitefulness in this town."

Carrie Smalls nodded her head.

"There is spitefulness everywhere," Mama said.

Sarah Jenkins tightened the thick woolen scarf wrapped several times around her neck. "Now, Candi, you know what Annie Mae is talking about. There *is* a pretty mean person in town that is poisoning folks. And if Abe can't find him, I say he ought to call in the State Law Enforcement people to help him out."

My father, Cliff, and my brothers, who had already endured Uncle Chester's visit, looked at one another. With their signals on target, the men marched in single file out into the hallway. They knew better than to get involved with Annie Mae, Sarah, and Carrie. Cliff muttered something about getting more coffee.

Mama pushed herself up onto her pillow as if she was prepared to defend the sheriff's crime-solving efforts. I have to confess I too had wondered what Sheriff Abe Stanley had been doing to track down the killer who had struck twice—and nearly three times—in Otis.

"Abe's doing all he can," Mama said, confidently. "These things take time to work out."

Annie Mae Gregory had by now walked over to a nearby chair and flopped her large body down into it. She sighed. "Well, I for one say that if Abe had caught the person when poor Hannah was killed, Nat would be alive today and you, well, you—"

Sarah Jenkins interrupted Annie Mae like she hadn't been listening to her. "Hannah didn't deserve to die like that, I don't care what people are saying."

Carrie Smalls, who had also made claim to a chair on the other side of the empty bed, scolded, "Now, Sarah, Hannah had her faults, we all know that!"

"Hannah had more than faults." I remembered my earlier thought that she might have known that somebody would kill for her land. "She had an enemy, big time!"

Annie Mae Gregory looked at Mama as if to

suggest that even the good Candi Covington had an enemy that she had pushed so hard he had finally tried to kill her. "Doesn't matter what you do to a person, there's no reason to kill, now is there, Candi?" Annie Mae asked.

Whatever Mama's thoughts on the subject, she ignored Annie Mae's question. Instead, she asked, "Do either of you ladies remember Leroy Mixon's son?"

"Of course we do," Carrie Smalls answered. "He was kind of sickly like his Mama."

"Reeves kept stowed up with a cold like I do," Sarah Jenkins said, feigning a cough. She fished around in her enormous purse for a cough drop, pulled out two boxes, chose the cherry-flavored.

"Stella always had to purge that boy," Annie Mae added.

"Is the boy still around these parts?" Mama asked.

The three women looked at each other and laughed. "Child, Reeves has been gone from home for years," Sarah Jenkins told Mama.

"That boy was one of those people who leave home and never look back," Carrie Smalls said firmly.

"Didn't even come to his Daddy's funeral," Sarah Jenkins said as she pulled a handkerchief out of her purse.

Annie Mae Gregory shook her head. "Leroy

Mixon wasn't exactly the kind of daddy you'd care much about."

I cleared my throat. "Have any of you seen Reeves Mixon lately?" I asked.

Nobody answered my question. The three women were silent. All three stared at me, without a word.

I tried another direction. "Have you heard that anybody has seen him?" I asked them.

Annie Mae Gregory shook her head. So did Carrie and Sarah. "Reeves was fifteen, sixteen when he left home," Annie Mae said. "That was over twenty years ago. I reckon that'll make him . . ."

"Thirty-five," I said. "You wouldn't happen to know which direction Reeves took when he left the area, would you?"

The women laughed. "Course we do," Carrie Smalls said.

"He's somewhere in Florida," Sarah Jenkins said.

"My sister's boy said he ran into Reeves a few years back," Annie Mae Gregory told us. "It was in Daytona. Or was it that place where the mouse is at?"

"Orlando?" I asked.

"Someplace in Florida." Sarah Jenkins said it firmly. "Reeves's down around there someplace."

Mama yawned, this time closing her eyes and letting them stay closed. Carrie Smalls rolled her eyes and sighed hard, but then she stood and walked toward the door. "It's late," she announced. Sarah Jenkins and Annie Mae Gregory promptly fell in behind her. "I guess people will be glad to know you're all right, Candi," Carrie told Mama. "Glad to know that you know who tried to poison you."

Mama opened her eyes. *"No, I don't,"* she said, knowing that nothing she could say would stop this trio from spreading untruthful information throughout the county.

"Course you do," Carrie Smalls said as she passed across the threshold into the corridor.

Annie Mae Gregory didn't speak, she just nodded her head knowingly, her chins wobbling.

"I don't understand you," I said to Mama in exasperation after the women had gone. "They talked about you behind your back, practically accusing you of murder, and you treat them like they're diplomats."

"That's a good analogy," Mama said.

"You can't make me believe it doesn't bother you that they suspect you of poisoning Miss Hannah and Nat," I said.

"Not really, but it's because I've got the upper hand," Mama confessed.

"Mama—"

"Simone," Mama interrupted, "I've convinced Calvin Stokes, Judge Thompson, and Abe to keep Hannah's will a secret for three more weeks."

"Why?"

"Because after you told me about what they were saying about me, I know that those three will spread so many lies about me all over the county, I won't be able to hold my head up."

"Who cares what they say? It's the person who tried to kill you that you should be worried about."

"I can find that person better if people don't know about the will," Mama insisted. "I won't have to spin my wheels defending myself."

I nodded. But the truth was that I wasn't as sure about Mama's rationale as she was.

CHAPTER
TWELVE

The next morning things seemed a little more hopeful. For one thing, Mama, who'd had a good night's sleep, seemed almost her old self again.

Dr. DeFoe visited her early, around five. While he examined her, I took the opportunity to look for Gertrude. She had mentioned the day before that she would be on duty early this morning. I wanted to check to see how she was coming with the list of hospital workers I'd asked for. I still wasn't convinced that somebody who worked at the hospital wasn't behind Mama's poisoning. That list would be the first step in finding out who that person might be.

But Gertrude was hedging. She hadn't done

anything toward getting me the list. I made her promise to work on getting it.

When I got back to Mama's room, Dr. DeFoe had gone on to his next patient. Mama was sitting up. Sheriff Abe stood next to her bed.

"Meant to come more oftener," he was saying when I entered the room. "This whole mess has got me jumping like a grasshopper."

Mama nodded.

"I was in Columbia yesterday meeting with the State Law Enforcement people about Hannah's and Nat's deaths. DeFoe called to tell me that you were finally conscious, that you were going to pull through."

Mama seemed satisfied with the sheriff's explanation of his neglect. "Did you get anything important from SLED?" she asked her old friend and sleuthing partner.

"DeFoe told me that he had sent the stuff he pumped from your stomach to the lab by a courier. Since I was there, I went to the lab directly. I pressured them a bit to get them to analyze it so quickly. Usually takes longer. Speaking of longer, good thing you came back to the hospital that night," Abe said. "DeFoe said you might not have made it if you hadn't."

"I would have never returned if I hadn't gotten that phone call," Mama said.

"Who called you?" the sheriff asked.

"I don't know who I talked to, but she said she was calling for Trudy Paige. If Trudy hadn't told that person that I was waiting for her at the Country Café, well—"

Abe scowled. Abe is a thin man with soft gray hair at his temples, deep lines in his face, and a mouth that turns down to show a bottom row of teeth. "I'll put Rick to hunting down Trudy Paige." Rick was Abe's deputy.

"I've got information on Trudy." I decided that this was something I wanted to be a part of. "She used to work right in this hospital. That is, until she quit right after Nat died."

"Trudy told me she hadn't quit," Mama said. "Told me that she still works here."

Abe shook his head. "I'll get to talking with the people here at the hospital. It shouldn't be too hard to track her."

"What about Reeves Mixon?" I asked.

Abe looked confused. "Reeves who?"

"Never mind about Reeves," Mama said. "We need to find Trudy."

"Yeah," Abe said, easing toward the door. "That girl set you up, all right."

"Wherever you find Trudy, let me know," Mama told him.

"I'll let you know as soon as I put my hands on her," Sheriff Abe assured her, and I knew he would keep his promise. He looked at Mama again, as if to assure himself that she was okay, then, with a nod, he left.

"Now that we've got Abe searching for Trudy," Mama told me, the moment the sheriff was out of hearing range, "we've got to find Reeves Mixon."

"You *do* think Reeves has something to do with this whole thing?"

"I think he might have wanted his land back," she replied. "We've known all along that Hannah inherited that land from Leroy, but we didn't know about Stella Gordon or her son Reeves. It's something we must look into."

One thing still puzzled me. "Why didn't you want me to tell Abe about Reeves?" I asked.

"Abe will have his hands full finding Trudy. Besides, there ain't no law against Reeves leaving home twenty years ago, is there?"

"Okay," I said reluctantly, "I'll call Sidney later this morning. Ask him for some more time off to stay with you."

"No, don't do that," Mama said. "I'll be all right."

"Do you honestly think that I could do anything in Atlanta knowing that you're here at the mercy of a killer?"

"Dr. DeFoe thinks I can go home tomorrow. I'll need to rest. I don't imagine anybody will come into my own house to harm me," she retorted.

"How about you going to Atlanta with me? You can rest at my apartment."

"I don't think so," Mama said. "My home is where I want to be."

"Daddy, Will, and Rodney will feel better knowing that you're away from Otis for a while," I pointed out craftily. I knew Mama wouldn't want Daddy and my brothers any more worried than they had been.

"I'll think about it," Mama said absently, like what she was thinking about was something other than staying in my apartment in Atlanta.

On Tuesday morning, we took Mama home from the hospital. Will went back to Florida, and Rodney flew back to New York. Cliff and I were finally headed back for Atlanta.

"I'll run a paper trail on Reeves Mixon when I get back to Atlanta," I promised Mama.

"Abe needs to find Trudy. I'm going to make that woman tell me why she lied to me if it's the last thing I do," she said, her voice determined. A chill ran through me. The last time Mama talked to Trudy Paige, it had almost killed her.

"And Simone," Mama said, looking at me

soulfully. "We've only got three weeks, three weeks before the will is released to Probate."

"I know," I said, softly, suspecting that the release of the knowledge about the will was more threatening to my mother than the person who had tried to kill her. The idea that people here in Otis were gossiping about her was very hurtful to her.

I traced Reeves Mixon from the moment he left Cypress Creek when he was fifteen, twenty years earlier, to his first job, caddying at a golf club in Daytona. Once I got his Social Security number, the rest was easy. I checked for a driver's license, credit reports, tax and bank records. I had a lot of experience doing this kind of research, working for Sidney's law firm.

Six months after Reeves left Daytona, he'd moved to Orlando. A year after that, he showed up in Miami. There he stayed for five years. The next time he worked, it was in Orlando at one of the same golf clubs he'd worked at before.

Reeves hadn't married. At least I couldn't find a marriage license. And he owned no real estate. I searched not only the tax records of every county he'd lived in since he left Otis, but also all the surrounding counties. And he didn't own a car either: I checked motor vehicle records— no car tags, nothing.

The one thing I did discover was that Reeves

Mixon had a serious drinking problem. Hospital records came from all over Florida. He had been hospitalized many times for alcohol poisoning. Reeves was no social drinker; the man drank a lot of liquor and he drank it fast.

The last record came from Orlando Regional Medical Center. Reeves had been diagnosed as having cirrhosis of the liver; he'd stayed a few weeks and was released. His prognosis was poor. The report was dated in May, six months earlier. And there the paper trail ended.

Everything I'd learned of Reeves made me see him as a sad person. He was a loner, with no family. He wandered from place to place. He drank too much. He'd been in and out of hospitals and had finally ended up with a disease that would soon kill him. If it hadn't already.

I wondered whether a man with this kind of unstable history would be able to murder with such cold precision. But then I remembered that Reeves's father had killed his mother; it might be in the blood, I thought. And he certainly had a motive. He had been denied his mother's inheritance, the only thing Stella Mixon had been able to pass on to her only son, those two hundred and fifty precious acres.

For the first time in years, my brothers and I talked almost daily. They called me every day. Sometimes we did conference calls, all of us on the phone at the same time. Will and Rodney wanted to find the person who tried to poison Mama just as much as I did. I shared with them what I had on Reeves. "Social Security cards, driver's licenses, hospital records are my expertise," I told them. "I've done everything I know and I still don't have Reeves Mixon."

"I don't understand what you think he's got to do with poisoning Mama," Will said.

"I don't know if he tried to poison Mama or not," I said. "But I know we need to talk to him."

"I can go along with talking to him. What do we do to find him?" Rodney demanded.

"I think we should get a leg man, a private detective who could talk to people, locate him," I said.

"Then we'll get one," Rodney said. Rodney, as I said, is my practical brother.

"We'll split the cost," Will interjected. "A third each, okay?" Will is my thrifty brother.

I sighed. "Okay," I agreed, thinking how my share would blow my budget out of the window again. But then, Mama's life was worth more than anything I'd allowed to disrupt my cash flow in the past.

"Sidney's best detective is named Kilroy Seymour," I told my brothers.

"Get the best," Rodney said.

"He's expensive," I warned.

"You get what you pay for," Rodney said.

Will grumbled, but he finally agreed.

"I'll keep in touch," I promised before hanging up.

Sidney had met Kilroy when the detective had appeared as a witness in one of Sidney's cases. "I like that Kilroy Seymour," Sidney told me after the trial. "He's got a talent." What Sidney meant, I soon learned, was that Kilroy had a unique ability to look like either a businessman or a bum. Dressed in a suit, Kilroy could get in places that were inaccessible to most African-American men. However, when he dressed down, Kilroy could be any bum on skid row, a wino, a derelict, a man down on his luck. Kilroy had one shortcoming, however: When called to look like the average Joe Blow, he couldn't pull it off; he simply looked stupid.

Kilroy Seymour was a man in his early forties with a quickly receding hairline, a close-clipped beard, and a mustache. Although he wasn't heavyset, he did look like he was accustomed to a life of substance.

Kilroy was definitely our man, so I called him. He agreed to fly down to Florida right away to look for Reeves.

CHAPTER
THIRTEEN

It was Saturday morning, four days since I'd left Mama. I slept badly.

I rolled over and glanced at the radio clock. Six A.M. At seven, I was dressed, and was grabbing my shoulder bag, my jacket, and my car keys. I congratulated myself that I'd had the sense to get the Honda gassed up; I didn't want to stop until I'd reached Otis.

I was pleased to see how well Mama looked. Her golden-brown complexion was glowing, her eyes sharp.

After hugs and kisses, our conversation focused on my efforts to locate Reeves Mixon. "If

Reeves is the killer, how do you think he's tied in with Trudy Paige?" I asked Mama.

She shook her head. "That's what's got me puzzled."

"They could be in this thing together. They could be lovers," I suggested.

"Where would Trudy have met Reeves?" Mama asked.

I rubbed my forehead. "You know, I've grown to expect murder in Atlanta, but the town of Otis is so peaceful. Most people who live here have known each other all their lives. It just doesn't seem possible that a killer could be one of you."

"Simone, the one thing I've learned from traveling with your father is that evil is everywhere." Mama said it gently but firmly.

For a moment I didn't say anything. Then something crossed my mind. "What about Cousin Gertrude?" I asked Mama.

"What about her?"

"She promised to get me a list of hospital employees."

Mama shook her head. "Gertrude has been by to see me twice, but she never mentioned a list."

I was annoyed. "Then I'll have to remind her," I snapped, thinking that there was no sense in closing the book on the possibility that somebody who worked at Otis General Hospital could be the killer in Otis, South Carolina.

CHAPTER
FOURTEEN

On Monday morning, I called Sidney and asked for a few more days off. Reluctantly, he agreed. The reason for my action was an announcement Mama made the previous morning.

"Time is running out," she had said. "In two weeks, the whole county is going to know about Hannah's will, and—"

"The knowledge of the will isn't as important as finding your would-be killer," I interrupted.

"Simone, I know the two are related," Mama said.

I wasn't convinced. "What do you plan to do?" I asked.

"Trudy Paige is the key to who is behind the killings," Mama said. "I'm going to find Trudy!"

"Sheriff Abe is looking for Trudy," I said.

"I know that," Mama said.

"You don't need to be out tramping all over the place. After all, you may still not be strong."

"I'm as strong as I ever was," Mama said.

"Mama—"

"Simone, I'm not sitting in this house like a prisoner, expecting Abe or that detective friend of yours to find whoever is out there poisoning people."

"What can you do?" I asked.

"I can find Trudy Paige, find out who put her up to luring me to that café, and—"

"Okay," I conceded. It was clear that I couldn't talk her into staying safely locked up in the house until Kilroy or Abe came through. But every time I thought of Mama's last encounter with Trudy Paige, I felt a tightness in my chest, and it was hard for me to breathe. If Mama insisted on meeting up with Trudy again, I would be with her. "I'll call Sidney and ask for a few more days off."

Mama laughed. "Simone, you think I can't take care of myself."

"I think that woman is devious and—"

Mama's eyes twinkled; she was pleased. "I need you, Simone," she said, her voice sounding as if she realized that my concern for her life was genuine.

On Monday morning, my father went off to work. After breakfast, Mama and I visited the sheriff's office. Abe was sitting with his feet propped on top of his desk. "Glad to see you, Candi," he said when we came in. "Morning, Simone."

"It's good to be back out and around," Mama told him. "Are things the same as it was when we last talked? Have you come close to finding Trudy yet?"

Abe frowned. "You'd think that woman has fallen off the face of the earth. I've got an APB out for her, but nobody has reported seeing her since the Friday night you saw her."

"She's been missing since the night I got poisoned?" Mama asked.

"That's right," Abe said.

"I suppose you've talked to Trudy's people?"

Abe nodded. "I've talked to Trudy's people from all over this county. Even talked to a few in other states—the last anybody owns up to seeing that girl was the night you talked to her, Candi."

"At what time on that Friday night was she seen?" I asked.

"Around ten o'clock," Sheriff Abe answered. "That brother of hers, Clyde Paige, told my deputy that he drove by Trudy's house to borrow

175

twenty dollars. Clyde said Trudy declared she ain't had no money, so he left." Abe paused. "One thing for sure, if Trudy told Clyde that she was broke, she was lying."

Mama's eyes lit up with interest. "Lying?" she said.

The sheriff dragged his feet from the top of his desk and opened a drawer. He pulled out a zippered red wallet and handed it to Mama. She opened it. "This is the woman I talked to in the parking lot—*this* is Trudy Paige." She pointed to the picture on the driver's license inside.

"That's Trudy all right," Abe said.

"Where did you get her wallet?" I asked him.

"Rick found it on her front step," the sheriff answered.

Mama flipped through the rest of the wallet's contents. Inside, there were five twenty-dollar bills, a Social Security card, and a piece of paper with a little black bird drawn on it.

"One thing for sure," the sheriff continued. "Trudy did quit her job at the hospital on the very day that Nat died, just like you said."

"Another puzzle," Mama murmured. She was staring down at the little bird drawn on the piece of paper again.

"Now, don't worry, Candi. We're going to keep looking for Trudy. And I've got my deputy Rick keeping an eye on you. You may not see him all the time, but he's looking over your shoulders, you can count on that."

"Thank you, but you don't have to—"

"I promised James we won't let nothing happen to you again." Abe said it like he would brook no argument.

"The only way we're going to protect Mama is to find the person responsible for the poisoning," I told the sheriff.

"You be careful what you eat," Abe told Mama. "Watch everything and everybody around you, you hear?"

Mama nodded, but she was still looking at the drawing.

The sheriff turned to me. "Rick and I have talked to each person who works at Otis General. Except for Trudy, we haven't found a link between any one of them and Nat or Hannah, much less Candi. And the truth is that I don't think the arsenic came from the hospital."

I took a deep breath. I was suddenly weary of what seemed like another dead end. "Okay, but do you have a list of the hospital's employees? And can I have it?" If Gertrude wouldn't get the list for me, I'd get it this way.

The sheriff shuffled through a stack of papers on the top of his desk. Finally, he pulled out a sheet and handed it to me. "You can have it, Simone, but I don't see what good it's going to do you. And, Candi—remember what I said. You be real careful till we find out what's going on in this town."

Mama nodded and headed for the door. As I followed her outside, I quickly examined the list Abe had given me. When we were seated in the Honda, I asked, "Where to now?"

"I want to go to Uncle Chester's house," Mama replied. "I need to get the map and picture I found in Hannah's Bible away from him before they get lost. First, though, swing by the house. I'll take Uncle Chester a bowl of the turnip greens left from yesterday's supper."

We drove up in the yard in time to meet the mailman. He handed me an overnight envelope with an Orlando return address on it. I thanked him, then opened it. Inside were three photographs. A note was attached. It read: *"I got these pictures of Reeves Mixon from one of the men who frequents the boardinghouse. Hope they'll help——K."* The first picture was of a man who was dark, thin, with deep-set eyes and thick lips. His nose looked like it had once been broken. If this was Reeves, he looked closer to fifty than thirty-five. The second picture was faded. It showed a woman wearing a white cotton dress and a large straw hat. Her face was pleasant but her eyes held a strange sadness. The third photo was of that same woman with a sickly looking boy about five years old. Reeves Mixon, before time and life had aged him.

"This is from Kilroy," I said, handing the photos to Mama.

Mama smiled. "Your private detective came through for you," she said.

I nodded, satisfied that I'd finally been able to do something to bring closure to the horrible events of the past few weeks.

CHAPTER
FIFTEEN

Uncle Chester was sitting by his heater, his frail body wrapped in its usual mound of blankets. He wore a stocking cap pulled down to his ears.

The first thing Uncle Chester did was to eat all of Mama's turnip greens. After that, she showed him the pictures Kilroy had sent. Uncle Chester looked down into the man's face.

"He's the spitting image of Stella's Daddy, George Gordon," Uncle Chester said after he stared at the picture for a while. "You'd think this was George's boy instead of his grand-boy."

I handed Uncle Chester the two old pictures. "Is this Reeves's mother?" I asked.

Uncle Chester squinted. "Look like Stella to me," he said, handing them back.

Mama looked toward Cousin Agatha, who sat placidly in the corner of the room, knitting. "I've come for the map and picture I sent by James," Mama said, addressing her.

Cousin Agatha stood, set down her knitting, then silently left the room. When she returned she held the items in her hand. "If that photo is the Mixons' place, that house is only a mile down the road, near the Jamisons' wire fence. That fence separates the property—everything on the right side belongs to the Mixons," she told us.

"Belongs to Mama now," I said softly.

"What's that?" Cousin Agatha asked.

"Nothing," Mama told her. "I think me and Simone will drive down there."

"This is the best time of year to make the trip," Agatha said. "The road's grown up. During the heat or rain, a car could easily get bogged down. In this weather, ground is hard, frozen."

Mama nodded and motioned me toward the door. "I done told you to cook me some more lamb stew," Uncle Chester snapped, seeing we were leaving. "Don't come back here again until you do, you hear me, Candi!"

Mama chuckled. The turnip greens hadn't satisfied his desire for the stew. "I will, Uncle Chester," she promised.

Cousin Agatha stepped close to Mama. "I think Daddy is going to sign over the power of attorney to me," she whispered. "That talk you gave him when he visited you in the hospital set his mind working."

"Let me know if I can be of any help," Mama offered.

Cousin Agatha nodded, then shut the door, leaving me and Mama to the windy, cold air.

The dirt road wound through a heavy forest for half a mile before we saw the old house. We stood in front of its sagging remains, remnants of a wood-framed house, its chimney broken, its windows long gone. All was quiet, too quiet. The area seemed to have a weird force of its own, one that seemed to push us away.

Inside, the Mixon house was as cold as a morgue. I know it sounds odd, but I swear you could feel the pain, hatred, and fear in these musty rooms the moment you stepped inside them.

Beside me in the shadows, Mama gasped. And then I saw what she'd seen.

The dead man's arms reached toward us. There was a face, or what was left of the face, on top of the naked, bloated body. The eyes were mere sockets; the cheeks, lips, and chin had been gnawed and torn by furry predators; the mouth gaped obscenely. The throat had been sliced from side to side, like some creatures had made an incision so that they could feast upon it. My stomach filled with bile.

Tears streamed down Mama's face. "Simone, we've found Reeves," she whispered.

A fat raccoon ran past me and scampered out the door. I screamed. "Lord," Mama prayed, "please don't let no rats come squealing out here today."

An hour later, Sheriff Abe, Rick Martin, and the paramedics had joined us. I'd used my car phone to call Sheriff Abe. The medic wiped his mouth with the back of his hand and shook his head grimly. "No gunshot or knife wounds," he told the sheriff. "My guess is that he died from natural causes."

"Will there be an autopsy?" Mama asked.

Abe pulled out a handkerchief and coughed into it. "Always an autopsy, in these kinds of things."

"How long has he been dead?" I asked.

"Based on what we know, maybe three, four weeks."

"Weeks?" Mama asked.

"It's the cold, windchill's below freezing," Abe replied. "Keeps a body for a long time."

"Then he was dead *before* Nat was killed," Mama whispered.

"I reckon," the sheriff agreed.

"Isn't it strange that he'd come way out here in the cold to die?" I asked.

Mama frowned. "I don't see any car. How did he get here?"

The ambulance crew thumped by, carrying their stretcher and body pouch. "Did he have any ID?" I asked the sheriff.

"There's no need for ID. It's Reeves Mixon," Mama said. "There is enough left of him to tell that!"

The two paramedics grabbed Reeves's arms and legs like he was a sack of flour, and put him into the body bag. When the dead man was zipped up, they carried him out.

"We found keys in his shirt pocket, that's all. No wallet. But I'm sure the boys at the SLED laboratory can verify that it's Reeves Mixon," Abe said, watching them.

"Did you find anything else?" Mama asked him.

The sheriff's eyes narrowed. "Not a thing," he told Mama. "You expecting something else, something I don't know about?"

Mama shook her head. "No," she said. But I could see Abe didn't believe her. He knew Mama too well. So did I.

Rick Martin got out a camera and a tape measure.

Mama watched him.

"I reckon this as good a time as any to tell you," Abe said, looking at Mama. "Hannah's will has reached Probate. It's going public."

"But I thought I had another week," Mama said.

"Seems like there was a mix-up. It got put in a stack of other wills, and—"

Mama groaned. "Annie Mae Gregory, Sarah Jenkins, and Carrie Smalls will soon know about it."

Sheriff Abe rolled his eyes heavenward. "If I was you, Candi, I'd get rid of this piece of property fast as I can!"

"He's right!" I agreed.

Mama stared at me. She didn't answer.

"Uncle Chester was right when he said this land is filled with blood. Why don't you just give it away?" I said. "Maybe to the county."

"What would the county want with land out in the middle of noplace?" Mama asked.

"For a game preserve, a bird sanctuary, a state park. Giving it away might defuse the damage your three friends will do to your reputation," I said.

"Yes," Mama said, her mind clearly thinking about what I'd just said. "You may be right."

"Sorry about that will." Abe followed Rick to the door. "You ladies coming?"

"I want to stay and look around some more."

"Don't see why, Candi, but it's okay with me." The sheriff shrugged. "Be getting dark . . . don't stay too long."

Mama took her glasses off and rubbed her eyes. I turned to look out of the doorway, to watch the sheriff and his deputy drive away. The ambulance was bumping ahead of them down the dirt road. Mama started to walk toward the other room. Then she stopped. A thought seemed to come to her. She turned and walked back to the crumbling fireplace.

Shivering, I tucked my elbows close to my sides.

"Simone, help me in case rats come out," Mama said, as she started moving bricks from the pile that had fallen from inside the ancient chimney.

I shuddered. "There's nothing underneath there, Mama!"

"I saw something," she insisted.

"Maybe it was just a piece of Reeves's clothing."

I was shivering and couldn't seem to catch my breath. But Mama paid no attention to me. She was poking through the dusty old bricks and ashes. Then, suddenly, she pulled something free. "This must be the envelope Hannah wanted me to have!" she announced.

CHAPTER
SIXTEEN

The envelope that Hannah Mixon wanted Mama to have wasn't heavy or thick. It was weather-beaten and grimy, but it wasn't torn or decayed. Mama looked down at it in her hand, then up at me, a secret glint in her eyes. "Let's go home," she said almost like she was talking to herself. "We need to look at this in the light."

At the house, I made hazelnut coffee. Mama sat down at the kitchen table. After she'd studied the outside of the envelope for a minute in silence, she carefully tore it open. On it was handwriting that was small and cramped.

"Do you want me to read it?" I asked.

"No," Mama said. "I'll do it." Mama read aloud:

Lord, I wish my hands would stop shaking. I have to do this . . . before I meet my Mama, I have to do this!

The day was hot, sunny. I was prone to fever, the runs. Daddy came home smelling like dirt. He had that look that scared me. "I'm going to kick tail!" he said. Mama flinched. I crawled under the table.

Daddy rubbed his forehead. He punched Mama. The lick landed on the side of her head. Mama's eyes grew wide. She took a half-step. She didn't say nothing, she looked at Daddy, then at me.

Daddy's eyes narrowed. He shook his head. He slapped her again; this lick landed on her jaw. Blood gushed from her nose and sprayed the table, the floor. Its smell made me want to puke. Mama staggered, then, like cheesecloth, she dropped to the floor.

Daddy looked down at her and smiled. Mama's eyes were open. Blood and spit were coming from her mouth.

Daddy straddled her, his hand on her throat. Mama's mouth opened but she didn't say nothing. Daddy looked straight into Mama's eyes until her body stopped twitching.

Then he stood up, got the bucket of wa-

ter, and threw it in her face. Mama didn't move.

The sheriff came. Daddy told him Mama had a fit, had fallen and hit her head. The sheriff asked me. I told him what Daddy told me to say. Mama had a fit, I said.

Daddy buried Mama. A week later, he married the widow down the road, Miss Hannah Wescot. Miss Hannah and her son moved in with us.

Daddy kept kicking my tail until I was fifteen, until I ran away. Miss Hannah told me that he died, but the pain didn't die with him. Mama's pain won't die!

Mama's eyes prey on me, haunt me, follow me. I wake up, screaming, then I'm scared to go back to sleep. Mama's eyes are there when I'm awake too, in the reflections of the mirror, in windowpanes, in pieces of glass. . . . Even when I drink, I see Mama's eyes.

Lord, I wish I could do this myself. Today is the day. The person I'm dealing with ain't got no conscience, ain't scared of nothing. . . . This will cleanse my soul. The land belonged to Mama. It should have been mine! If both Miss Hannah and Nat dies before I do, I will get Mama's

land back. Mama will forgive me. I've
given her land to the person who promised
to kill Miss Hannah and Nat for me.

When Mama's voice faded away, I struggled
to visualize Reeves Mixon the way he'd looked in
the photograph that Kilroy had overnighted us.
But all I could see in my mind's eye was the face
of the bloated corpse Mama and I had found. I
took a shaky breath, trying to erase the sickening memory. "Sounds to me that Reeves made a
deal with somebody to kill Hannah and Nat."

"Yes, it does," Mama murmured.

"It appears that Reeves believed that once
Hannah and Nat were dead, the land would be
his to will to that person as payment for their
murders."

Mama nodded.

Daddy, who had come into the house while
Mama was reading, cleared his throat. "Reeves
is dead. Hannah and Nat are dead, too. That
land belongs to you now, Candi."

"Yes, but the killer seems to have decided that
Mama must die!" I pointed out.

"Over my dead body!" Daddy exclaimed.

"There's something there that doesn't jive," I
said. If Mama was murdered, surely the killer
wouldn't get the land. "Since Miss Hannah

willed it to Mama, the Mixons' land would go to us—Mama's heirs, isn't that right?"

"Simone, baby, you're on target," Daddy said, looking at Mama for a response. "So, Candi, why is the jerk trying to kill *you*?"

Mama shook her head. "James, I don't know. Meanness . . . anger . . . Whoever it is has already murdered two people and has gotten nothing for his efforts. I suspect he's pretty frustrated."

For a moment, nobody said anything.

"Mama," I finally said, "I hate to bring this up, but I've got to go back to work in two days. Sidney isn't going to let me talk him into any more emergency vacation days."

"I understand," Mama said. But I thought I heard a little melancholy in her voice.

"It's going to be hard for me to work knowing that a killer is on the loose in town and you're at the top of his hit list."

"Don't worry about Candi," Daddy told me. "She'll be all right."

Easier said than done, I thought. "Do you have any idea of who is at the bottom of these murders?" I asked Mama.

Mama's face changed. Her familiar expression said a light had flickered on in her mind—Candi Covington was on to something. When she spoke, though, her tone was doubtful. "There's a

192

thought that keeps surfacing, but I can't find a place for it," she said.

"How about sharing that thought with us?" I asked, glancing toward my father. I felt better. Despite what she had just said, I knew that my Mama had at last found a thread that would lead her to the answers and maybe defuse the talk that was sure to spread about Hannah Mixon's putting Mama in her will.

"I keep thinking," Mama said, "that the person who bargained with Reeves to kill Hannah and Nat knew how much that property was worth before he struck the deal."

"Trudy Paige might have stumbled onto that information," I said.

"Abe is doing a poor job in finding that woman, and I've got a mind to tell him so!" Daddy snapped.

"Now, James," Mama said gently. "Abe's doing his best. And as for Trudy knowing about the Mixon land, I suppose it's possible." Her expression was troubled.

"It wouldn't be hard for her to find out about it," I pointed out. "All she'd have to do is check the county tax records the same as I did."

"I suppose," Mama murmured. "But Nat didn't know about that land until *after* Hannah's will was read, remember?"

"We all know that Nat was one short of a six-pack," Daddy said.

"He didn't know much of anything," I agreed.

"I suppose it's possible Trudy found out about the land, but there still has to be a link from her to Reeves, and—" Mama stopped in the middle of her sentence.

My father and I waited but Mama didn't say any more. "Speaking of Reeves," I said. "I guess I should page Kilroy, tell him that we've found Reeves."

"Good idea," Daddy said as he headed for the front door. "I'll see you two later."

Mama sighed.

❦

Half an hour later, Kilroy returned my call. "We've found Reeves's corpse," I told him.

He sighed. "That explains why I can't find him," he said.

"He was dead even before somebody tried to poison Mama," I said. "Long before I hired you."

Kilroy sighed again. You could tell he'd really hoped Reeves Mixon was our killer. "I've learned one more thing," he said. "Don't know how much good it'll do you, though."

"What's that?"

"The person who took Reeves from the hospital six months ago to take care of him . . ."

"Yeah?"

"It was a relative."

My heart beat a little faster. "Male or female?" I asked.

"Don't know. Just know that Reeves told one of the other patients that one of his kinfolk was going to take care of him."

I took a deep breath. "Mama would be interested to hear that," I said before I hung up the phone.

"I think," Mama said, after I had told her what Kilroy had told me about Reeves, "I'm going to invite Sarah Jenkins, Annie Mae Gregory, and Carrie Smalls for supper tomorrow."

"Mama, you know what those women think about you. Now that the will has become public knowledge, they're probably spreading all kinds of lies about you," I protested.

"Simone, I need to know a little more about the Mixon family, and there's nobody in this county that knows more about its residents, alive or dead, than Annie Mae Gregory, Sarah Jenkins, and Carrie Smalls!"

CHAPTER
SEVENTEEN

The next afternoon, Mama's dining room table was set with the handmade crocheted tablecloth. The china and crystal were from Germany. My father had gotten them for her when he was on one of his Air Force tours, before he retired. Rodney had sent the silver from New York for our parents' twenty-fifth wedding anniversary. He'd also talked Will into buying the matching serving pieces and coffeepot.

Mama loved setting a beautiful table.

The food: turkey and corn bread dressing, cranberry sauce, fried chicken, string beans mixed with new potatoes, rice, collard greens, yellow squash, fried okra, succotash, corn bread. For dessert there was red devil cake and coconut cream pie. My mouth watered, just looking at the array in the kitchen.

Despite the tension Mama felt about what these women were doing to her reputation, when Sarah Jenkins, Annie Mae Gregory, and Carrie Smalls arrived at our house, they sat at a table designed to reward them for the information they were willing to share.

Carrie Smalls was dressed in a tailored black dress with a lace collar. Her long hair draped her shoulders. Annie Mae Gregory wore gray, a long, flowing polyester dress that accented her large frame. Her piercing eyes shone. Tonight, she kept a Cheshire cat smile on her face during the meal *and* she kept talking with food in her mouth.

Sarah Jenkins had on a two-piece navy blue suit. Her white blouse had tiny white buttons down the front of it.

Clearly, all three women were dressed for a feast. I could only hope Mama wouldn't be their main course.

Daddy and I wisely kept silent. At first Mama, seated at the foot of the table, spoke in an officiating manner that was unnatural, like she was making a speech. "I wanted to thank you ladies for visiting me while I was in the hospital."

The three women stared, like they didn't know the Candi Covington who was talking to them.

Then Annie Mae Gregory spoke. "It was nasty of somebody to try to kill you, especially after Hannah willed you all her property," she said, grinning.

Sarah Jenkins leaned forward. "I don't believe I know anybody who was *almost* killed. Most folks either get killed or—"

Mama took a deep breath like she was mustering up courage to go on with her dinner. Then she opened her mouth to say something. But Annie Mae Gregory, who now had a piece of turkey hanging from the side of her mouth, beat her to it. "My God, Candi, what kind of Christian woman are you? How could you have accepted Hannah's land?"

Mama was in a terrible dilemma; for an instant she actually seemed lost for words. She needed to get information from these women, but she didn't like the idea of having to defend herself against their questions. The thought that she might have hurt somebody seemed too much for her. I could see that she was biting back the impulse to argue, the strong desire to set these noisy women straight. But when she answered Annie Mae Gregory, her voice was impressively unemotional. "I haven't done anything to anybody," she said evenly.

Annie Mae Gregory's fat jaws shook like

Jell-o. "You know folks are saying you talked Hannah into giving you her land."

Mama struggled to maintain her grace and poise. But I saw defiance spark in her eyes. "That's just not true," she told Annie Mae.

Frail Sarah Jenkins swallowed a tiny mouthful of collard greens. "That's what people are saying. Course we ain't saying we agree with them, but you know, where there's smoke there's fire!"

I shifted in my seat because I could see that Mama was about to lose her temper. I decided to change the conversation before she did. "I suppose you ladies heard about Hannah's step-son," I said.

Now, all three women stared at me. "No." Sarah Jenkins rubbed her chest like she might have indigestion. "What happened to the boy?"

"The sheriff found Reeves Mixon dead yester-day," I told her, delighted that I had knowledge they didn't yet have. "He was in the old house on the Mixons' homestead."

The women sat up straight, their fingers laced tightly on top of the tablecloth. "I declare," Sarah said.

"Tell us all about it," Annie Mae said.

I felt a burst of energy, like something pro-ductive was really going to come out of this meal. Sarah Jenkins began rubbing her stomach, trying to make herself belch. Mama got up and went into the kitchen. When she came back, she seemed to have regained her composure. "Candi," Sarah Jenkins said when Mama had sat back down, "did I tell you that I've got high blood pressure?"

"You told me about your heart problem," Mama told Sarah. "When did you find that out about your blood pressure?"

"Dr. Clark told me day before yesterday. Course I knew it all the time!"

Mama smiled a little but said that she was very sorry to hear it. "My ankles swell, my feet hurt, and I get these headaches," Sarah Jenkins continued. Carrie Smalls glared at her.

Mama took a deep breath. "I know you ladies told me that Hannah's people are dead—"

"Died out like most people right after the war," Sarah Jenkins said heartily.

"I was wondering about her husband's people," Mama went on. "She had four husbands, didn't she?"

"What do you want to know about them?" Carrie Smalls asked.

"I was wondering whether any of her husbands had children by another woman?" Mama asked.

There was a momentary silence.

"None that we know of," Sarah said, looking back and forth between the two other ladies.

"Like we told you, Hannah's first husband died young. Her second husband spent too much time gambling to do much of anything," Sarah Jenkins declared.

"It surprised everybody when Hannah turned up pregnant with Nat," Annie Mae Gregory said.

"Her third husband, Richard Wescot, never fathered no children himself, though his brother Claude had his share," Carrie Smalls said.

Mama looked interested. "How many children did Claude have?" she asked. There was a glint in her eyes.

"Two girls," Carrie Smalls said promptly.

"Betsy Wescot married a Fennell boy from Low Branch. The other girl never married," Sarah Jenkins said.

"Betsy still in Low Branch?" I asked.

"Betsy got killed in a car wreck last year," Carrie Smalls snapped, like that was information I should have known.

Annie Mae Gregory looked past me, or at least I think she did. She tilted her head in the way that makes her look a little cross-eyed. "I watched those girls grow up. Me and their Mama, Josie, use to pick peas on Old Man Parker's place some years ago."

Annie Mae mashed potatoes and string beans together into a mush, then stuffed a wad in her mouth. "Betsy was all right but that Raven, people said she wasn't wrapped too tight. Something wrong with her brains from birth, I think."

Carrie Smalls broke in, her fork poised in midair, another wad of mashed food on its tips. "Now, Annie Mae, I heard that about Raven but I knew that girl. She had a problem, but she wasn't as crazy as most folks made her out to be."

Annie Mae Gregory chuckled. "I declare, Carrie. If what people say is true, that girl set fires to her own house, and killed dogs and cats."

Carrie Smalls frowned in honest defense of the gossip against the Wescot girl. "I talked to Abe and her people about that, and they told me that one of Michael's boys set those fires," she insisted. "And those animals, they died a natural death!"

Annie Mae Gregory's eyes widened and I could have sworn that she looked embarrassed. She wasn't used to a contradictory story. "Since you keep disputing anything I say and you claim you know that girl, *you* talk!" she snapped at Carrie. "I might as well keep my mouth shut!"

She didn't, though; she stuffed more string beans and mashed potato into it, instead.

Carrie Smalls threw Annie Mae Gregory a contemptuous look, but went on eating and didn't answer.

For a time, nobody said anything.

"Candi, get me some Epsom salts," Sarah Jenkins said.

Mama left the room again. When she returned she carried the box of Epsom salts and a large glass of water. We all watched Sarah Jenkins take a heaping spoonful of salts, watched her drink the entire glass of water. She belched, then reached immediately for another big helping of collards and corn bread.

Carrie Smalls's eyes darkened. She had some feeling for this girl. There was something about her she liked. "Raven used to come to my house when she was a young miss, used to write letters for me, read my mail for me, things like that. Mind now, it's true she had a strangeness about her, but I watched her grow out of that."

Pain flickered across Sarah Jenkins's narrow face like lightning. Her chest seemed to tighten, her shoulders shook a little. After the spasm had passed, she nipped a piece of corn bread between her thumb and index finger. "People said Raven was spooked. Said a gypsy marked her when she was a child."

Carrie Smalls sat up straighter. "People say that 'bout anybody they don't understand. That girl needed somebody to take up time with her, that's all!"

For a while nobody said anything more. The

women were preoccupied with their heaping plates of food.

My father, who had wisely been silent for most of the meal, emptied his glass of wine with one swallow, and then poured himself another. "Does Raven live around here?" he asked casually.

Now, Sarah Jenkins looked at Daddy. Her eyes were enlarged behind the rimless bifocals that hung on her bony face. She belched softly. "Raven has been gone away from around here for years now, ever since she finished school."

Carrie Smalls leaned forward smugly. You could see she was about to disagree with Sarah. "Raven came home for Hannah's funeral. She stopped by my house and we had a long talk. She's doing fine, real good now!"

I cleared my throat. "Was she here for Nat's funeral, too?"

Carrie Smalls shifted in her chair, took one tiny sip of iced tea, then another. "I don't reckon she came home. Not much of anybody attended *that* funeral."

Sarah Jenkins glared at her.

The atmosphere would have continued strained, but Mama reached over and patted Carrie's hand. "I'd like to get in touch with Raven Wescot, talk with her about the property Hannah willed me. After all, now that both Nat

Mixon and Raven's sister, Betsy Fennell, are dead, Raven is Hannah's nearest kin, don't you think?"

Carrie Smalls nodded. "I suppose Raven could be considered a kin, yes."

"I'm for doing the right thing," Mama said.

Carrie Smalls hesitated, thinking. "I don't reckon Raven would mind if I gave you her address. . . ."

Mama flashed a smile.

Another silence followed.

"Are there any others of the Wescot family still living in these parts?" I asked.

Carrie Smalls glanced at Mama with a bit of caution, then reached for the bowl of collards. "There are some distant cousins in Darien."

Mama's eyebrows raised. "What can you ladies tell us about Hannah's last husband, Leroy Mixon?"

Sarah Jenkins cleared her throat; her chest rattled. She started coughing.

"You all right?" Daddy asked.

She nodded. "It's my windpipe," she said. "It'll be all right soon as it's clear."

We waited.

After a while, Sarah Jenkins continued. "Ain't much to know about Leroy Mixon. He was a drinking man, mean and—"

I cut in. "I heard he made it a practice to beat Miss Hannah?"

Carrie Smalls gave me a direct look. Her dark eyes were cold, almost piercing. She rested her elbows on the table and waved her fork in the air. "There's not a man in these three counties who would try to beat up on Hannah Mixon!" she said indignantly.

I took a deep breath and tried hard to keep my voice polite. "I guess I'm wrong. Maybe what I heard was that Leroy Mixon beat up on his *first* wife."

Annie Mae Gregory nodded. "That's a fact. People say Leroy killed Stella just so that he could marry Hannah."

Carrie Smalls nodded, chewing on a buttery piece of corn bread. "I knew Leroy all his life. He *was* mean enough to kill!"

Sarah Jenkins folded her arms across her bony chest. She took a deep breath that sounded like a strangled moan.

I glanced at Mama. She refused to give me eye contact. Daddy snickered.

Annie Mae Gregory spoke, the flesh under her large jaws swaying like autumn leaves in a slight wind. "Stella Gordon was too good for Leroy. If Stella's Mama and Daddy were living, they'd never have let Leroy court her."

I sipped from my glass of iced tea and eyed

Mama, who finally slid a look in my direction. She reached for the silver coffee urn at her side, poured coffee into a china cup. "You know," she said, matter-of-factly, "since Hannah and I were neighbors, I wish that I would have gotten to know her better."

"Don't fret about that, Candi," Annie Mae Gregory said. "Not many people got close to Hannah Mixon. What surprises us, and I reckon it surprises everybody in town, is that she left *you* all of Leroy's property. The Hannah Mixon I knew was mean enough to try to take it all with her!"

And both Carrie Smalls and Sarah Jenkins nodded.

CHAPTER
EIGHTEEN

The telephone rang. Sarah Jenkins, Annie Mae Gregory, and Carrie Smalls looked around the table. Mama glanced at her watch, then got up to answer the phone. After a moment, she put her hand over the receiver. Her eyes had filled with tears. "Uncle Chester has had another heart attack. He died on the way to the hospital!"

Three hours later, we sat in Cousin Agatha's front room. "It happened so quickly," Agatha kept sobbing. "He was signing his name on the power of attorney when he got his first pain. I suppose I should have taken him to the hospital right then, but he said not to bother 'cause it stopped hurting him. He started to sign his last name when the second pain hit him. I knew it was bad this time so I bundled him up, put him in the car, and headed for the hospital. He . . ." Her voice trailed off into a sob.

"It was best the way it happened," Mama soothed. "He didn't suffer."

I wondered if she was thinking of the painful deaths the town of Otis had seen in recent days.

One week later, we buried my great-uncle Chester. The sky was gloomy, the air wintry cold. A few flurries of snow whipped across our faces as we stood in the cemetery.

The drive to the Cypress Creek Baptist church had been short and no one spoke during it. Mama, Daddy, Cliff, and I walked to the front of the church and sat down. The church was built of cinder block; it was bitterly cold inside. Hundreds of people came to the funeral, people from all over the country, as well as the county. The women, in their dark dresses, cried as they walked slowly up the aisle to view Uncle Chester for the last time in the open coffin.

An hour later, when Uncle Chester's coffin descended into the earth, I couldn't help but think of how much of his life he'd spent trying to protect what appeared to be his eternal resting place.

Daddy, dressed in a navy suit, a white shirt, a dark tie with small burgundy comma figures, stood at Mama's side. Cliff wore a gray European suit that complimented his muscular, dark-complected body. He stood next to me, holding my hand.

After the burial, we went back to Cousin Agatha's house. The potbellied stove was red, and a long table was full of food, a good portion of which had been cooked by Mama.

Cousin Agatha immediately sank into her chair, obviously tired from the ordeal. A few of Daddy's other cousins acted as servers so that we could sit around the fire and talk, since funerals are our way of visiting informally.

Sarah Jenkins, Annie Mae Gregory, and Carrie Smalls had already taken their seats. All were eating when Annie Mae Gregory looked at Mama. "Candi," she said, her mouth full of fried chicken, "I know people are talking about Hannah leaving you all that land but, child, you're doing good. You ain't even scared of whoever it is that's been trying to kill you!"

Everybody suddenly seemed to need to cough. Daddy's cousin Tishri, the sister of a twin, tried to dilute the impact of Annie Mae Gregory's statement by asking Daddy's cousin Gertrude a question. "How much arsenic *does* it take to kill a person?" Tishri demanded.

I bit my lower lip and watched Mama. But if talking about her brush with death bothered her, she didn't show it. Gertrude answered Tishri's question. "Not much," she said, cheerfully.

Tishri looked around the room. She seemed pleased that everyone's eyes were on her. "How long does it take before you feel the effects of poison?" she asked, satisfied that she was the center of attention.

Gertrude looked like she had been put on the spot. "I don't know," she said, her tone unsure. "I just work at the hospital, I'm not a doctor."

Tishri now turned to Mama. "What kind of treatment did they give you, Candi?"

"They pumped my stomach," she replied.

"How did it make you feel?" Tishri asked, her eyes searching Mama's face.

Mama looked around the snug room filled with relatives, friends, and neighbors, people who eagerly wanted to hear her tell the story. It was the kind of a thing that set nerves on edge, that made you realize how much people like hearing about the evil that happens to other people. "My stomach felt like a knife was slicing through it!" Mama said reluctantly.

I glanced around the room: They waited to hear something more. "The nurses around told me that you were vomiting, and had diarrhea with blood," Gertrude said, when it was clear that Mama wasn't going to continue.

Mama nodded. "I was hoping I didn't have to tell all that."

We laughed. My mother wasn't the type you'd imagine throwing up or having diarrhea. It just wasn't the thing you expected of Candi Covington.

Gertrude's voice boomed above the laughter. "I remember a story that one of the doctors told me," she said. "A man was admitted to a hospital complaining of weight loss, severe gastric problems, hair loss, numbness, and skin rash. The doctors ordered test after test, but they all came back negative. They were about to send the man home without knowing what was wrong with him when one doctor overheard nursing students talking. One girl, who read mysteries, jokingly said that the patient's wife must be poisoning him with arsenic. The doctor wrote the order to test the man's arsenic levels and was shocked when the test came back positive. The man's wife *had* been giving him poison every morning in his coffee!"

"You ain't trying to say that it was James that poisoned Candi, are you?" Sarah Jenkins demanded loudly as everyone else laughed.

Whatever emotions Daddy had bottled up

against these women now broke loose. He wasn't laughing. For a second, watching his face, I actually thought he was going to hit this silly woman. He shook his finger in front of her watery eyes. "Sarah Jenkins, have you lost your mind?"

Mama and I rushed to Daddy's side. "Now, Daddy, calm yourself. Miss Jenkins didn't mean that. Did you?" I asked.

"Calm down, James," Mama added.

Sarah Jenkins shook her head. She was scared. Her face told everybody in the room that if she had ever *thought* James Covington capable of hurting his wife, she was very sorry she'd *said* it.

"Now, James." Carrie Smalls came to her friend's assistance. "No sense losing control, you know. Sarah didn't mean no harm."

"James," Mama said. "Carrie is right in what she's saying."

But Daddy was livid. "I had better never, *ever* hear anything like that said again!" he shouted.

Sarah Jenkins didn't say anything, but she was trembling. Carrie Smalls spoke again. "We all know that you'd never do anything to hurt Candi."

This was the last time I remembered hearing from either Sarah Jenkins, Annie Mae Gregory, or Carrie Smalls that day. To be honest, they were so uncommonly quiet, I don't even remember them leaving the house.

Somebody passed around a plate of deviled eggs. I glanced at Mama, who looked at the platter, shook her head, and handed it to the lady next to her.

Right after that, Daddy's first cousin from Philadelphia, Fred Covington, got to his feet. He cleared his throat loudly. "We might as well have this out here and now," he declared. "It's my opinion that land is dirt. The only good it does you is when you're dead and gone like Uncle Chester. Money is what's for the living, plain and simple!" Fred looked around at the gathered family and friends, glaring.

Cousin Agatha squirmed in her chair. "If you're insinuating that we sell the Covington land, Fred, it ain't going to happen. This land has been in our family since Reconstruction. And it'll stay with us until Christ comes again!"

Fred waved his hand dismissively. "What you're saying doesn't make any sense," he insisted.

Cousin Agatha spoke again. "Our people worked hard for this land, did without things they needed, suffered so that we could have it." Her voice trembled with emotion. Fred tried to cut her off, but she didn't stop talking until she had finished her speech. "As long as I live, it won't be sold!"

"Suffered for what? So you could have *this*?" Fred roared, pointing around the room. His eyes bulged. "Floors that are wooden, walls that are plywood that's been stained mahogany, chairs that will give you splinters if you sit too fast, a table with one of the four legs shorter than the rest?"

Daddy stood up, anger still in his voice. "Take it easy, no need talking about this place like that. As long as Agatha is comfortable . . ."

Cousin Agatha's usually timid eyes held their determination. "Mind you, I could use better," she told Fred, "but not at the expense of selling the Covington land."

"Corporation is what we've decided to do with the land, that's all to it!" Daddy added hotly.

The veins popped up in Fred's neck. He stuttered furiously. "I-I want my piece. I'm g-going to sell it."

I took a deep breath. How much scotch had Fred drunk since he'd arrived for the funeral?

"Sell to who?" I asked.

"What?" he roared, turning to stare at me like he'd never seen me before.

"Who are you going to sell your portion of the land to? That is, if you get it?" I repeated calmly.

Fred glared at me. "T-There's a man who's

215

trying to buy land. I've talked to him and he's offering a good price for it, way above what it's worth!"

"Who is he?" Mama asked. There was an odd look on her face. "What's his name?"

"It's not really a man," Fred replied hastily.

"Then who?" Daddy demanded impatiently.

"It's a company. A corporation."

"What would a company want with acres of rural land?" Mama asked.

"They want to farm the timber," Fred answered. "The money ain't in cotton, watermelons, or soybeans anymore. The money is in *timber!*"

"What company?" I asked. "What corporation is buying up land around here?"

Fred's look grew blank. "I-I don't know. I just know this company wants to buy land around here so that they could farm timber. I-I ain't got nothing against that. And you shouldn't either!" he roared at poor Cousin Agatha.

"Well, I do have something against it," she snapped, showing more spunk than she'd ever shown while Uncle Chester was alive. "I don't care if a plow never touches the Covington land again! No company's getting it!"

"How much is this company offering an acre?" Mama asked Fred.

Fred hesitated. "Two hundred fifty dollars.

Maybe two seventy-five," he said. "But I got the idea they'd give more for a quick deal," he added greedily.

"I don't care if they give a thousand dollars an acre, we're not selling," Cousin Agatha retorted.

"K-keep your land to be buried in, if that what's you want. I-I want my Daddy's part and I've got a right to it!" Fred bellowed, veins bulging again. I was glad Gertrude was in the room, just in case he had a stroke.

Cousin Agatha folded her arms across her breast. "Can't be split," she said, satisfaction in her voice. "I done put it in a corporation and that's all to it!"

"Can't be! Uncle Chester wouldn't never sign the papers for something like that," Fred roared.

"Well, he did," Cousin Agatha replied. "Before my Daddy died, he signed the papers. Ain't that right, James?"

Daddy nodded. "It's legal and all. We've had the lawyer look it over, everything has been fixed up. Nothing more can be done about it."

Fred's mouth twitched. The sweat poured from his forehead. "What good is having all this land when—"

Cousin Agatha cut him off. "Calm down, Fred. I knew you wanted money. So I've got it set up that the timber on the land will be cut

217

every ten years. The money from that will be divided among us."

Fred scowled. "What good will that do us *today*?"

"The timber hasn't been cut since I was a boy, almost fifty years ago," Daddy said.

Cousin Agatha beamed. "It's going to be cut soon as the weather breaks, and it should net us all a little money to do something with."

"How much money are we talking about?" Fred asked anxiously.

Cousin Agatha smiled. "Enough, I hope, to get me a better house to live in," she told him with satisfaction.

Tishri turned to Mama, who seemed lost in her private thoughts. "Why don't you sell those two hundred fifty acres Hannah Mixon left you to that company Fred just told us that's looking to buy land?" she asked.

"I'm not going to sell that land," Mama said firmly. "I'm going to give it away."

"Give it away! For God's sake, why?" Fred looked like Mama had just uttered a string of swear words.

"Because I don't want to profit from it," Mama answered evenly.

"Who are you going to give it to?" Tishri asked.

"The county," Mama said. "They're going to make it a nature preserve."

Fred stomped toward the front door, pushing through the roomful of people. "That's stupid," he boomed. "You people are too crazy about dirt. Obsessed with dirt!" he spat out.

"I don't think you should give that land to the county," Cousin Agatha told Mama. There was a pleading in her voice. "Give it to somebody in Hannah's family. People around here believe that land should stay in the family!"

Mama looked stunned. Cousin Agatha's words seemed to have hit her like a brick. She stared at Agatha as if she was the only person in the crowded room.

"You all right, Candi?" Daddy asked, concerned.

But I recognized the look on Mama's face. "She figured out what has been happening," I said. "Isn't that right, Mama?"

"There is a bond between family and their land," Mama whispered. "She wasn't trying to *kill* me, she was trying to *scare* me into giving her back her family's land!"

CHAPTER
NINETEEN

Inside the car, Mama made her announcement. "I want to stop by Abe's office. Can you drive me, Cliff?"

Daddy made a face. "What you need Abe for?" he asked.

"I need his help," Mama said. "I need Abe to convince Judge Thompson to allow me to give Hannah's acres to another person."

"Another person?" I asked.

"I thought you were going to give the land to the county for a nature preserve?" Cliff asked.

"I've changed my mind," Mama told us. "Land should be kept in the family. Agatha reminded me of that—it's the way folks do things around here. It's what I've been expected to do all along!"

The sheriff and his deputy were in their office. "I'm glad you stopped by," Abe said, when we walked in the door. "Hunters found Trudy Paige's body in the woods behind her apartment house this morning."

Mama thanked Sheriff Abe for that information. Then she explained her theory about the poisoner. A little over an hour later, we all left the office. Sheriff Abe, Deputy Rick Martin, Daddy, Cliff, and I agreed to help Mama with her scheme. She had worked out the details of a trap to catch a killer.

Two weeks after that, Cliff and I were once again back in Otis. I must admit what we'd planned to do was scary. The only thing that made Mama's plan halfway all right was that Sheriff Abe and Deputy Martin would be in the next room.

"It's possible," Cliff had warned Mama, "what you get won't stand up in court."

Mama had shrugged. "It'll have to do. There's no other way."

"It won't stand up in court even though the

sheriff and Rick Martin will hear it?" Daddy asked.

Cliff shook his head. "I doubt it," he said.

"Maybe the killer will confess," I said.

"If the killer is as ruthless as Miss Candi thinks," Cliff had replied, grimly, "I doubt that, too!"

❦

Mama had a set table again. Her crocheted tablecloth, her china, silver, crystal. Everything was perfect. Mama was ready for her guests and it showed.

The menu: homemade relish tray with pear relish, roasted turkey with herb gravy, baked country ham, peach catsup, corn bread dressing, steamed rice, marinated vegetable salad, candied sweet potatoes, turnip greens, brandied cranberries, yeast rolls, and butternut pound cake with caramel sauce. Just looking at that table made my mouth water.

Judge Thompson had finally agreed to Mama's petition, and Calvin Stokes had notified Hannah's niece Raven Wescot that Mama wanted to give her the two hundred and fifty acres of land; Mama, Calvin had told Raven, felt the land belonged to somebody in Hannah's family, not to her.

Exactly at one o'clock, the front doorbell

rang. A few minutes later, Mama walked into the dining room. Both Raven Wescot and Moody Hamilton followed behind her.

Raven looked different than she had the first time we'd seen her, the day she'd been with Nat in Mama's kitchen. I remembered her light skin, but her lustrous hair was no longer in long thick cornrow braids; today it hung loosely over her shoulders. Her large black eyes were clear and intelligent; her features looked sculptured, almost aristocratic. She smelled of Chloé perfume, a scent I particularly liked. Still, something about her struck me as odd. I think it was her body language. Every gesture and motion seemed exaggerated. "This is a beautiful table! The food looks delicious!" she said, her voice soft, breathy.

Mama normally loves it when someone admires her cooking but today something told me that it didn't much matter. "Thank you," she told Raven. "I'm glad that Calvin was able to convince you to join us."

"I was happy that you decided to give up our land," Raven said. "I'm glad you've come to feel, like most folks around here, that heirs' property belongs to the family!"

"I really didn't want it," Mama said. "It's right that it goes to Hannah's kin."

Moody Hamilton, who hadn't looked into

Mama's eyes since he had arrived, glanced at her now, then turned away. He looked very uneasy.

Later, after we were all seated, and the food was being passed around the table, Mama turned to Raven. "I understand that you're Hannah's niece through her third husband, Richard Wescot. Is that right?" she asked politely.

Raven held a fork full of turnip greens in mid-air. She didn't answer at once. She shifted in her chair and seemed to want to make us wait for her explanation. "I'm kin to Hannah through Uncle Richard but I was kin to Hannah before he married her," she finally told Mama. "Hannah's second husband, Charles Warren, was my mother's brother."

"Nat's father was your uncle, too?" I asked.

Raven nodded. "Hannah made Nat use the Mixon last name but Nat was really a Warren like all my Mama's people," she said. Raven smiled, then ate her forkful of turnips. We waited. "Besides that," Raven continued, "Hannah's fourth husband's first wife, Stella Gordon, and my mother were sisters."

"I was under the impression that Stella Gordon didn't have any brothers or sisters," I whispered to Cliff. The unsettled feeling in my stomach intensified.

There was silence. "My mother was an outside child. Old man Gordon never admitted to fathering her. Still, my Mama was a Gordon," Raven said firmly.

Daddy, who had just swallowed a piece of country ham, nodded knowingly. "One thing about those old people, they didn't mind sowing seeds wherever they found fertile ground."

Raven cut her eyes, unamused.

Mama smiled and looked at Moody. He sat, staring morosely down at his hands, his fingers interlaced and knotted on Mama's best table-cloth. "Moody, I've known you for years," she said. "I had no idea that you were any kin to Hannah or Nat!"

Raven's head jerked toward Moody. Moody didn't say anything. Finally, Raven spoke. "Moody is my son," she told us.

Moody kept staring at his hands. "My grand-mother in Darien raised me," he said, as if he needed to explain. "I just got to know Raven a few months ago when she came home for a visit just before Hannah died."

Raven's gaze drifted away from Moody. "I told you I had to finish nursing school, had to get a job." She paused. "But all of that is behind us now," she added cheerily.

From that point on we talked about land that had been handed down from generation to gen-eration and how difficult it was for families to keep it intact. Daddy did most of the talking.

"Forming a land company and incorporating it is the thing to do," he said. "That way, no matter how many generations come and go, the land will always stay with the family."

Moody, who didn't eat much, took long pauses between bites. At one point, he raised one hand to his mouth, put a knuckle to his teeth, and gently chewed on it. Raven gobbled up four or five bites in rapid succession, saying little, but agreeing with most of what was said. She seldom looked at her silent son. Suddenly her eyes were scanning the table.

Mama was the first to notice. "What are you looking for, Raven?" she asked.

"Turnips," Raven replied. "There's no more in the bowl."

Mama smiled. "There's plenty in the kitchen. Give me your plate and I'll get it for you," she said. Raven handed her the plate; Mama excused herself and headed off toward her stove.

Daddy kept talking about land. "There are people," he told us, "who think that selling land and getting the money is the best thing. Grant you, you can't eat land, but it's still money. Take for instance this property, this house. If I ever got in tight for some cash, I could borrow on it, use this house and land as collateral."

Raven didn't say anything, but the expression on her face showed that she was more interested in what Mama was going to bring out of the kitchen than what my father was saying. Mama came back and handed Raven her plate. "I don't know the last time I've eaten such good greens," Raven told her.

Daddy grinned. "Candi knows how to lay it on you," he agreed, reaching for the bowl of candied sweet potatoes.

"I'm glad you like them," Mama told Raven. "Eat up, there's plenty more in the kitchen."

I hid a smile, wondering whether it would dawn upon Raven that if there was so much food in the kitchen why was it that it hadn't been put on the table.

Mama was reading my mind again: She shot me one of those looks as she sat down. "What are you going to do with Hannah's acres?" she asked Raven. Her eyes went to Moody, who looked increasingly miserable.

Raven filled her mouth with a large portion of the turnip greens. She shook her head and pointed to her mouth. Mama, who looked earnest and concerned, waited. "I'm going to sell it," Raven said, as she pushed her fork into the plate of greens again.

I could have croaked. "Sell it?" I exclaimed, putting down my knife and fork and picking up my napkin. "I thought you'd want to keep it in the family."

Raven shook her head. "Me? No." She filled her fork again. "I like money, the things money can buy. I've already got a buyer!" she said. We watched her chew, swallow, then gulp the third and final fork of greens. Her plate was empty again. I wondered if she was going to ask for more.

But seconds later Raven's greedy, determined expression became one of uncertainty. "Those greens . . . don't seem to be agreeing with me . . . feel like I've got indigestion," she mumbled. Beads of sweat were popping out on her forehead.

Mama adjusted her glasses low on her nose. Her mouth formed a grudging line, like she was offended by Raven's sudden illness and Raven's claim that her sickness must have come from Mama's cooking.

Raven blew out a breath, then shoved her plate back. Her light skin turned ashen. She tried to get up from the table but stumbled back into her chair. Cliff shot a look at me, but nobody moved to help Raven, not even Moody. He just sat staring at her like he'd never seen her before and what he saw he didn't much like.

"Are you hurting?" Mama asked her, her voice calm.

Raven made a funny noise, deep in her throat.

A tear sprang from one of her eyes and trickled down her cheek.

The air in the room suddenly seemed thick. Under the table, I placed my foot on top of Cliff's and applied pressure. His expression didn't change.

Raven shivered, as though a current shot through her. Then she doubled over, clutching her stomach and moaning. Nobody moved.

"I've poisoned you," Mama told Raven serenely. "The same as you poisoned me."

Raven's body was shaking. Mama looked sterner than I can ever remember seeing her. *"I've given you a good dose of arsenic,"* she said, coldly.

Moody didn't move, didn't say a word. He stared at his mother.

"Raven should be dead in a half hour!" Mama told us, folding her napkin and laying it neatly on the table beside her plate. "That is, if she doesn't tell us why she killed Hannah and Nat and Trudy Paige, and why she tried to kill me!"

Moody took a deep breath. The young man looked like his relief was as great as if he had been trudging along an ocean floor with billions of tons of water pressing down on him and had abruptly been transported to dry land, where only air weighed on his shoulders. He looked like he knew that he himself had finally escaped death.

Raven's dark eyes widened. "I didn't . . ." she started to say when another pain hit her. She gasped. "For God's sake, get me to the hospital!"

Mama shook her head. She carefully smoothed her napkin. "That's why you lured me to the hospital that night, isn't it?" she told Raven. "You knew I'd get treatment right away, knew they'd get the poison out of me before I died of it. You *needed* me to live, so I'd give you that land, isn't that right?"

"No!" Raven hollered. Her eyes glittered like a sick animal's.

"I'm not as benevolent as you," Mama continued. "You'll be dead before I call the paramedics."

"Moody!" Raven screamed, appealing desperately to her son.

Moody shook his head but didn't look at his mother.

"You are all murderers!" Raven gasped. "Killers . . . !" Another pain silenced her.

Nobody moved.

"Well, isn't it nice," Mama said serenely. "A dinner fit for a king. Or should I say a dinner fit for a *killer*?"

Raven's body shivered. The sweat poured

from her skin. She gagged. Without hurrying, Mama went into the kitchen and came back with a foot tub, which had a small amount of water in it along with a dash of Lysol. She set the tub down in front of Raven.

"I'm dizzy . . ." Raven complained.

"You're a nurse," Mama told her. "You know the next thing is convulsions and then a coma."

Another tremor shook Raven's body.

"Okay," she wheezed. "I admit to it!"

"Admit to what?" Mama asked.

"I did it!"

"Did what?"

"*I . . . killed Hannah and Nat!*" she cried.

"And Candi?" Daddy asked.

"I didn't want to kill you," Raven gasped. She looked pleadingly into Mama's eyes. "I just wanted to scare you . . . into giving me the land."

Mama nodded. "I know that now. But surely you didn't have to poison me to do that. You could have just asked. It was never really my land. I would have given it back to Nat. But you killed him, too."

Raven's eyes widened. Her face was slick with sweat. "Get me to the hospital," she pleaded, "before I die!"

Sheriff Abe and Rick Martin entered Mama's dining room. "You won't die," Mama told Raven as the sheriff started reading her her rights. "I didn't put *that* much of the digitoxin that I got from Gertrude in my turnip greens!"

In the silence that followed after the sheriff and Rick Martin led Raven to their patrol car, which was parked behind our house, Cliff cleared his throat. "Like I said before, I don't know if any of what she just said under duress will hold up in a court of law." He shook his head.

"Now that we know she's guilty, maybe we can find something more concrete," I said.

"I'll tell you what she did." Moody's voice was so faint we almost didn't hear him.

CHAPTER
TWENTY

Sheriff Abe took Raven Wescot to Otis General Hospital. There her stomach was pumped. Then, the sheriff took her to jail. The next day he drove her to the State Penitentiary in Columbia. Moody Hamilton turned state's witness against his mother; six months later, Raven was tried and found guilty of the murders of Hannah and Nat Mixon, Trudy and Mama's attempted murder; the trial lasted all of three days.

When it was over, she was sentenced to life in prison without parole. Moody was sentenced to five years' probation for his role in the assault on Nat's life.

Mama prepared one of her feasts. The menu: chicken breasts with marmalade, a garden vegetable lasagna, baked potato salad, mustard greens, okra, rice, gravy, string beans, glazed carrots, and brown rice. Dessert: A pumpkin-pecan pound cake and a lemon cream pie.

Will and Rodney came home to celebrate with Mama, Daddy, Cliff, and me. Sheriff Abe, Rick Martin, and Moody had been invited, too. So was Kilroy, who'd driven down from Atlanta for the event.

The meal was well on its way when Rodney brought the table talk around to murder. "Mama, if I'm out of line asking you to tell us about the poisoning and how you got on to Raven, then excuse me. It's just that I missed the trial, and there's so many things I don't know about what actually happened."

Will put his fork down for a moment. "Yeah, it'll be helpful if you start from the beginning, Mama. You know, give us details."

Mama glanced around her table. Her gaze stuck on Moody briefly. Moody shifted in his chair.

"I don't know if Moody wants to hear us talk about it," Mama told my brothers.

Daddy did a neck roll, like he was trying to relieve tension. "I can't think of what hasn't been already said, what with the trial and all," he said.

Moody's voice was so low we all had to lean

forward to hear him. "It's all right with me," he told Mama. He shifted in his chair again.

Mama sipped from her coffee. Then she said, "Moody, you are to be complimented. I know how hard this was for you. Without your testimony, the evidence against Raven wasn't very strong."

"I know," he murmured.

Mama smiled and nodded. "You said at the trial that you only knew your Mama, Raven, a short time. How was that?" she asked.

When Moody looked up, I changed my opinion of him. He wasn't the sly, fluid man I'd made him out to be when I'd first met him in the club's parking lot. This was a young man with a sense of innocence and compassion.

"Raven left me with my grandma when I was a baby. As far back as I can remember, the only Mama I knew was Grandma," he told my mother.

"Talk is that your grandma was a good woman," Mama said.

I'd never seen Moody smile before. His smile lit up his whole face. "Grandma treated me good every day of her life!" he exclaimed.

Daddy coughed. "You were good to her, too," he said.

"I did my best by her. I was all she had."

Moody hesitated. "At least that's what I thought until Raven showed up!"

Nobody spoke.

"It was a real surprise when she came claiming to be my mother. Grandma had never mentioned her. Every time I'd asked about my Mama or Daddy, Grandma would say she was all the Mama and Daddy I needed. After a while, I started thinking they must be dead. When Raven told me that she was my mother and that she had a plan that would make us a lot of money, I was surprised. She told me she needed my help. She had met one of our kinfolk in the hospital where she was nursing. He was dying, she told me."

"Orlando Regional in Florida was where Reeves Mixon had last been seen," Kilroy explained to us.

"Raven told me that Reeves's land had been stolen from him, and that after him, she was the rightful heir to the land since Grandma was Stella Gordon's half-sister." Moody shook his head. "Grandma never mentioned Stella Gordon to me. I had no idea that we were kin until Raven came."

"Your grandmother was an outside child," Daddy said. "Sometime a person like that claim kin, sometime they don't."

Moody glanced at Daddy, then looked away.

You could see that knowing his grandmother had been born out of wedlock still made Moody uncomfortable. He shifted in his chair. "Raven told me that Reeves wanted his land to go to a Gordon before he died."

"But he never got his wish; he died before Raven had finished her work," Mama said softly.

Moody nodded. "The next thing I heard Miss Hannah was dead, had been poisoned. Raven went to the funeral, hung around with Nat, acting like she was a friend. I didn't think too much about it."

Mama looked at the sheriff. "Abe, what made you decide to have an autopsy done on Hannah?" she asked.

The sheriff put down his fork. He'd been feasting greedily on Mama's garden vegetable lasagna, his favorite, but now he was working on dessert. "The undertaker's assistant called me. I wasn't too convinced. I know how these young people are, but I ordered the autopsy anyway. Then I stopped by Hannah's house, where I found the receipt showing that she'd paid Calvin for some legal work. Calvin told me about the will, about Hannah's land going to you."

"I was surprised you didn't talk to me about it," Mama said.

The sheriff picked up his fork again. He was on his third piece of Mama's pumpkin-pecan pound cake. "I ain't never suspected you of doing anything wrong, if that's what you mean," he told Mama. "I just wanted to get information."

Mama smiled.

Daddy had an annoyed look on his face. I decided to change the subject. "Why did Reeves write that letter? The one about Stella's death?"

"I guess he wanted Miss Hannah to know that he was going to get revenge," Mama told me. "When Hannah got Reeves's letter, she did what she thought was right. She willed the land to me so that Nat wouldn't get killed for it. But Reeves died without knowing that."

"How did the note get behind the chimney in the old house?" Rick Martin asked.

Mama cut him another slice of cake before she answered. "Hannah hid it there for me to find. I guess she didn't want it in her house in case Nat stumbled across it and found out what she knew. She figured I'd go out to the old house right away, thought I'd want to look over the property I'd inherited. She didn't figure on the wind knocking down some more bricks in that old chimney so that I almost didn't find it."

"And Reeves, how did he get there to die?" Cliff asked.

Moody coughed. "I didn't mention this at the trial because nobody asked, but . . ."

We waited. But when I glanced at Mama, I

was certain she knew exactly what Moody was going to say.

"The truth is," Moody continued reluctantly, "Reeves died in Florida, in Raven's house. She didn't want to fool with burying him so she drove him home, here to Otis, then got me to help her take him out to the old house. She said the wild animals would eat him. She said nobody would ever find him."

I shivered, remembering the sad, bloated body in the decaying house.

"That woman *is* mean, ain't she?" Rodney murmured. My brother Will, whose mouth was full of lemon cream pie, nodded.

"After Miss Hannah died, I wanted to warn Nat to watch out 'cause Raven was after him."

I snapped my fingers. "That night we saw you go to Nat's front door!"

"Yeah, but I didn't want to believe that Raven had done anything to old Miss Hannah, so I turned around and went back home. When I asked Raven about Miss Hannah's death, she admitted to it. She told me that since I'd helped her handle Reeves's dead body, I'd just as well go all the way and help her kill Nat since I was a part of what she had already done!"

"So you waited for him in the dark that night?" I asked.

Moody's narrow face looked regretful. "When

Nat came home, he was drunk. I hit him two times with that hammer, but then I smelled his blood and I couldn't hit him again!"

I made a point of making eye contact with Moody. "Nat told us that the person who hit him smelled funny. What was he talking about?"

Moody turned his head slightly. He shuddered. "Chloroform. Raven used it on Miss Hannah to knock her out before she injected the arsenic. That night, she tried to put a rag soaked in chloroform over Nat's mouth, but he fought so hard, she couldn't do it. Like I said, after the second blow, I just dropped that hammer and ran. Raven figured I hadn't killed Nat, so she picked up the hammer, hit him again, then followed me." He shivered again. "After that night, I told her that I couldn't help her anymore. Killing people ain't my nature."

Cliff cocked his head in Moody's direction. "How did she poison Nat when all those people were around him in the Melody Bar?"

"I was in the club at the time. Nat was pretty drunk, he was spending money, buying drinks for everybody. I saw Raven slip inside, saw her stand next to him, then slip back through the crowd. A few minutes later, he fell to the floor."

Mama frowned. "I can only imagine her fury when she discovered that after those two killings, she couldn't get the land after all."

"Raven *really* wanted to kill you, Miss Candi," Moody said. "But she decided the only way for her to get the land was to *pretend* to be trying to kill you so that you'd be scared into giving it to Hannah's kin. She was sure that sooner or later, you'd track her and give the property to her."

For a moment, nobody spoke.

Moody sighed. "I hadn't seen Raven since Nat died. She must have slipped in and out of town. But then she came to my house. She was so happy. You'd finally found her, she told me. Calvin Stokes had contacted her."

"So you don't know when she hooked up with Trudy Paige?" Mama asked.

Everybody at the table stared in Mama's direction but it was Sheriff Abe who spoke. "When the hunters stumbled upon Trudy's body we found a note in her pocket. She had been offered a hundred and fifty dollars to play a trick on Candi," he told us. "A black bird was drawn as a signature on the note, the same bird we found on the note in Trudy's wallet."

Mama frowned. "That trick she got paid for was to lure me to the café and then back to the hospital."

The sheriff nodded. "SLED's forensic verified that Raven was with Trudy when she died," he said. "That evidence is what the prosecutor used

241

to convince the jury that Raven murdered Trudy, too."

Daddy leaned back in his chair and raised his arms, lacing his fingers so his hands were resting across the top of his head. "That land didn't mean anything to Raven, but it meant everything to poor Reeves. I reckon when Raven told him that she was his mother's niece, the poor boy thought if she had it, it would once again be in the Gordon family, where it belonged."

"You don't think Reeves knew that Raven was going to sell the land, do you?" Cliff asked.

"Heavens, no," Mama replied.

"What a trap you set for Raven," I told Mama. "I liked the way you didn't put much food on the table. It took all I could do not to ask for more."

"How did you know she'd come here for dinner?" Will asked. "I think if I was a poisoner, I would have been too *scared* to eat anybody else's food."

Mama laughed. "First, I knew that Raven had no idea I was on to her. And I knew she wanted that land bad enough to kill three times for it. To make sure she'd come, though, I told Calvin to make it clear that her coming to my house for the meal was an important part of me giving her the land. It was the best way to ensure that she'd show up," Mama said.

"She was glad for the invitation," Moody said.

"Fortunately, Raven had a good appetite," Mama said.

"Everybody knows what a good cook you are, Miss Candi," Moody said. "I told Raven it was a privilege to sit at your table."

When everybody at the table enthusiastically agreed, Mama smiled. These were the kind of compliments that pleased her.

"Mama, what are you going to do with that land now?" Rodney asked. "It does belong to you."

Mama crossed her arms under her bosom. "I'm giving it to Moody here," she said, her eyes resting thoughtfully on him. "It's Gordon land. His grandma was a Gordon. It's rightfully his."

To everybody's surprise, however, Moody disagreed. "I don't want it," he said quickly and too loudly. "It's tainted. I don't want no tainted land!"

Daddy threw back his head and laughed. "I'm with you, boy. Land like that needs cleansing."

Mama looked at Daddy, then studied Moody for a moment. "If you're sure that you don't want it, I'll go with my first inclination. I'll give it to the county, let them use it as a nature preserve, so *everybody* can enjoy it."

Moody smiled for the second time. "That's fine with me," he said, satisfied. "I've got enough taxes to pay on Grandma's piece of property in

Darien. Lord knows she'd turn over in her grave if she thought I'd sold that or lost it for taxes."

Kilroy reached for another giant helping of lemon cream pie. "Miss Candi," he said, "I don't know what you've put in this food, but if it makes me sick, it's worth every bit of the pain and the pumping of my belly."

Daddy started rubbing his stomach, like he does when it's more than satisfied. He reached over and touched Mama's cheek. "Baby," he said, his voice warm, tender, "you've outdone yourself on this one, you've *really* outdone yourself this time!"

And Mama smiled.

If you enjoyed Nora DeLoach's MAMA STALKS
THE PAST, you won't want to miss the latest mys-
tery starring Candi Covington and her daughter
Simone, MAMA ROCKS THE EMPTY CRADLE.

Look for MAMA ROCKS THE EMPTY CRADLE
in hardcover from Bantam Books at your favorite
bookstore in December 1998.

AND TURN THE PAGE FOR AN EXCITING
PREVIEW.

MAMA ROCKS
THE EMPTY CRADLE

by Nora DeLoach

CHAPTER
ONE

I'd failed.

Frustration hung over my head like a halo. The task hadn't been hard. My boss had given me a routine assignment, one that normally took me less than a week to do. "Run a paper trail, find this witness; our client swears he exists," he'd said. Then he gave me a name, a description, and an approximate age.

When I didn't come up with the person, my boss, one of Atlanta's best defense lawyers, plea-bargained for his client. Then he boarded a plane from Hartsfield to take a European vacation.

I sat, staring at a diploma that I'd taken so much pride in earning, and thinking about the day I'd interviewed for the position of paralegal in Sidney Jacoby's research department. I'd already had five such interviews in less prestigious law offices without a hint of a job offer.

Except for my urge to flick dandruff from his shoulders, I swiftly sized Sidney Jacoby up to be pretty cool. Sidney looked down at my résumé, then back up to meet my eyes. "Simone Covington," he said, as if he liked the sound of my name.

I nodded.

"Graduated from Emory, I see."

"Yes," I said.

"Are you going on to law school?"

"No," I admitted. "I like the legal research."

Sidney laughed. "I like the research myself," he admitted. "Did a lot of that when I was in law school."

"You were a paralegal?" I asked, surprised.

"Yes," he said, shaking his head, his dark brown eyes twinkling in a way that made me sure he could be warm with compassion at one moment and cold at the next. He leaned back in his seat, and crossed his fingers in front of him. "Nobody can tamper with the truth," he continued. "If you dig deep enough, peel off all the layers of appearances, cut away through the lies, and strip through the absurdities, you'll find the truth, Miss Covington."

I smiled.

"The adrenaline you feel from the experience is priceless," he said.

My eyes widened. I believed the man, believed he shared my passion for getting to the heart of things.

"I suppose we have a gift," I heard myself say.

"Yes," he agreed, as if I had said something profound. His eyes twinkled. "And don't you ever take that gift for granted, Simone Covington."

The next day, Sidney Jacoby telephoned me and made me a generous offer.

I've worked for Sidney for five years now, five

years in which he had never taken a vacation. Oh, he'd planned to get away, all right—every detail of a six-week tour of Europe from the time the plane leaves Hartsfield until it lands in London, he had planned. But he had never done it.

When I admitted that I'd come up empty-handed in my search for our witness, Sidney didn't say much. But I was sure he was disappointed. I suppose that's why I was thinking about the day he had interviewed me, remembering our mutual belief in digging until we got what we sought.

Still studying my diploma, I reached for a box of Godiva chocolates and my phone and called my mama. "Sidney's gone on vacation," I told her.

"Good, then you can take some time off, too—come home," she replied.

"Just because Sidney is out of town doesn't mean that there isn't any work for me to do."

"It's midsummer. Sidney needed a vacation and you do, too."

"When I told Sidney that I couldn't come up with his witness," I told Mama, "he stared like he saw something in me that he'd missed all these years—"

"Simone," Mama interrupted. "You're doing it again. Overreacting. It's normal for people to take vacations in the summer and Sidney is normal. Besides, if that witness existed, you *would* have found him. Sidney and I both know that!"

I swallowed. "Maybe that's why he didn't push me to keep looking," I said, my spirit lightening.

Mama's voice was softer. "Forget the case. Take a week's vacation and come home—I need you."

"You want help to solve another murder?" I asked, and laughed.

Mama laughed, too, a light musical sound. "Not

this time," she told me. "I'm scheduled for surgery first thing Monday morning."

I sat up straight. "What kind of surgery?" I demanded. "What's wrong with you?"

"Nothing serious," Mama replied. "I'm just having bunions removed from both my feet. I'd planned for James to go with me to the hospital—"

"Hospital?"

"It's outpatient surgery, Simone," Mama said. "Anyway, you'd be a big help to me. With Sidney out of the country for six weeks, you can spare a week of your vacation, can't you?"

"Cliff—" I started to say.

"You and Cliff will have at least two weeks left to do something together. But, tell you what I'll do," Mama said, and I knew I was about to be bribed. "You come home on Friday, you and I will shop and cook on Saturday, then Cliff can drive here and have Sunday dinner with you, me, and your father."

My boyfriend Cliff is a divorce lawyer who is working hard to become a partner in his firm. The thought of how much Cliff and I both loved Mama's cooking whirled through my mind. "Cliff has been pretty busy with another one of his detachment clients," I said.

"Divorces seem to be plentiful these days," Mama commented.

I nodded although she couldn't see me. "It's worst when a client thinks her divorce lawyer should be at her disposal every minute of the day."

Mama didn't say anything.

"How long will you need me?" I asked again. My spirit rose at the thought of eating another one of my mama's meals.

"A week," she said.

"A week," I repeated, thinking that Sidney would surely expect me to use *some* of my vacation time while he was gone, especially to take care of my mama.

My mama's name is Grace, but she's called Candi because of her candied sweet potato complexion.

My parents are originally from Otis, South Carolina. They got married right out of high school and my father joined the Air Force. After a career of thirty years and the birth of my two brothers (Rodney and Will) and me, Captain James Covington retired and he and Mama moved back home to Otis, a town of five thousand people.

On Saturday morning, we were in Winn Dixie shopping for groceries when the baby's wail rang through the aisles. It sounded like somebody had stuck a hand down the infant's throat and squeezed its intestines.

I flinched. Mama held her shopping list in one hand, a can of mushroom soup in the other. She was saying something about sodium when the child's second scream broke her concentration. She glanced in the direction of the cry. "Something is wrong with that child!" she said, softly, putting the can of soup back on the shelf.

A voice over the loudspeaker suggested that shoppers visit the produce section . . . watermelon, grapes, and peaches were on sale. Then one of my favorite songs by the Manhattans began to be piped through the store.

Mama eased her shopping cart toward the juices; I hummed along with the music.

The baby screamed again, the sound as sharp as a police siren. Mama looked at me; I threw her a look of reluctance, but it didn't do any good. She was going to see what the matter was with that child and that was all there was to it. I shrugged, then followed her toward the noise.

On the next aisle, near the canned vegetables, we spotted a woman who looked all of thirty years old, who smelled powerfully like the camphor used for canker sores. She was holding a baby and shaking it. The woman's skin was dark. She had small eyes, and a very large nose. As we walked toward her, she looked scared, almost terrified.

I glanced at the baby . . . it was beautiful, although its tiny face was as red as the labels on the cans of tomatoes that were on the shelf. It wailed again.

"Birdie Smiley, what's wrong with that baby?" Mama demanded.

Birdie stammered but she didn't stop shaking the baby in her arms. "I-I had no business—"

Mama interrupted impatiently, "That's Cricket's baby, Morgan. What have you done to that child?"

Birdie didn't look up. Instead, she began shaking the baby harder. The baby screamed.

"*Stop that!*" Mama shouted, then she snatched the crying baby from Birdie's arms. "If you keep that up you'll knock the wind out of her—she'll stop breathing!"

Birdie's body was trembling. Beads of sweat were on her forehead. "I-I ain't got no business keeping her . . . ain't got no business letting her come with me . . . I just remembered, I ain't got no business keeping *nobody's* baby!" The words poured from her mouth like a hot flood.

Mama was cradling the sobbing baby in her arms, looking down into its wide-open eyes. "Now, Morgan," she whispered. "Everything is going to be all right!"

"I ain't got no business keeping a baby," Birdie stammered. "Doctor told me I ain't got the nerves for it . . . ain't got no business . . . can't take care of no baby . . . won't do it again!"

The baby hiccupped and stopped crying. "I was at the hospital the day this baby was born," Mama said, as if talking to herself. "She had the brightest eyes, and when you talked to her, she paid attention like she understood exactly what you were saying."

I looked closer at Morgan. She was indeed enchanting. For a moment, I felt a strange inkling, like the prickle of an unfamiliar emotion. Morgan's eyes charmed me, too.

"Is Birdie some kin to Morgan?" I asked, thinking that such a nervous woman had no business taking care of this delightful baby.

"I don't think she is," Mama answered. "Cricket Childs, Morgan's mother, is one of my clients."

Mama works for the Social Services Department. "Then this beautiful child is the other side of the coin of a single-parent home," I said.

"I suppose," Mama replied, in a tone that told me that she didn't think my statement was relevant.

As long as Morgan held on to my eyes, I had to agree with Mama. This captivating baby girl looked almost a year old. She had thick black hair and a flawless milk-chocolate complexion. Her eyes were dark and bright, her mouth small and round. She smelled of Johnson's baby powder. But cuteness wasn't all there was to this little girl. There was something bewitching about that child's gaze.

Mama smiled down at Morgan, clearly having fallen in love. This baby's bright beckoning eyes had that kind of power. "I can't imagine Cricket leaving you, sweet child," Mama whispered.

Birdie Smiley stood anxiously rubbing her arm and staring at Mama and little Morgan when Sarah Jenkins, Annie Mae Gregory, and Carrie Smalls eased up quietly beside Mama. In Otis, these three women are jokingly called the "town historians" because they go out of their way to know everything about everybody in Otis. Mama actually finds them helpful. She calls them her "source."

I was surprised to see the ladies, but Mama glanced at them as if she'd known all along that they were in the store. "Ladies," she said, without taking her attention from the smiling baby, "it's good to see you."

"I told you," Sarah Jenkins said, her voice strong despite her pasty complexion and constant preoccupation with her health, "that was Cricket's baby hollering."

Annie Mae Gregory is an obese woman, whose body is the shape of a perfect oval and who has dark circles around her stonelike eyes; Annie Mae always reminds me of a big fat raccoon. When she looks at you a certain way, she appears cross-eyed. She asked Mama, her jaws shaking like Jell-O, "Candi, what are you doing with Cricket Childs's baby?"

"I ain't got no business—" Birdie Smiley muttered, as if talking to herself again.

Mama glanced up. "Now, Birdie, Morgan is just fine now."

Carrie Smalls is a tall woman with a small mouth and a sharp nose. She holds her body straight, like she's practiced so that her shoulders wouldn't slump—I've told Mama more than once that it's Carrie Smalls who gives strength to the three women's presence, who gives a measure of credibility to what these three say. Carrie Smalls looks the youngest; she dyes her hair jet black and lets it hang to her shoulders. Now she looked down into Mama's arms at the baby girl. "Where's Cricket?" she asked, in an authoritarian tone.

Just about that time, Koot Rawlins, a large woman known for being full of gas, swung into the aisle and belched. Koot's shopping cart was full of lima beans, rice, fatback bacon, and Pepsi. She nodded a greeting but kept walking.

I went back to staring down into little Morgan's face. "My friend Yasmine, the beautician, she had a party a few weeks ago—a young woman named Cricket was there who told me she lived in Otis. Could she be this baby's mother?" I asked.

Mama's attention shifted back between me and the baby as if she was surprised. "There's only one Cricket Childs that lives in this town, and she's Morgan's mother, yes."

Annie Mae Gregory shook her head impatiently. "Where in the world is Cricket now?" she snapped.

Sarah Jenkins looked around. "I declare, Cricket's got her share of faults—"

"Whatever Cricket's faults," Mama interrupted, "she's a good mother. I can personally vouch for her devotion to this child."

Carrie Smalls shrugged. "I reckon you think 'cause your job throw you to be with her that you know her better than anybody else. My question now is where is Cricket, and why is she letting her baby cause so much confusion in this grocery store?"

"Cricket isn't far," Mama said, convincingly. "She must have left Morgan with Birdie for just a few minutes."

Carrie Smalls motioned to her two companions that it was time for them to leave. "You work for the welfare, Candi," she told my mother. "You know better than anybody else that if Cricket doesn't take better care of her child, it'll be your place to take her away from Cricket and put her in a home where she'd be properly taken care of. A grocery store ain't no place to drop off a child—"

"I don't think it's fair to say that Cricket

dropped Morgan off in the store," Mama pointed out. "Birdie is taking care of the baby."

Carrie Smalls responded sharply, "There are times when Birdie can't take care of her own self, much less take care of a hollering baby!"

I watched the three women shuffle down the aisle toward the fruit and vegetables. But Mama ignored them. She was still staring at the baby in her arms. "We'll find your mama, sweetheart," she whispered. Her words seemed to hold the child's attention.

Suddenly, I decided I shouldn't be a part of this scene. Let me explain. I-I . . . well, I just don't have a very strong maternal instinct. Don't get me wrong, that doesn't mean I don't like babies—it's just that they don't turn me on like I'm told they are supposed to do!

Birdie Smiley, whose bottom lip trembled and who hadn't spoken since Sarah Jenkins, Annie Mae Gregory, and Carrie Smalls had moved on, now stepped backward, knocking down a few cans from the shelf.

Mama didn't look at Birdie. "Morgan," she was saying, "you are a pretty little thing, now aren't you?"

I remembered I wanted some Famous Amos so I turned and walked toward the cookie row.

A few minutes later, I was standing in the ten-items-or-less checkout line when I saw Sheriff Abe, his deputy Rick Martin, and Cricket Childs run into the store like they were going to put out a fire. Something was wrong.

In the back of the store, a crowd had formed around Birdie, Mama, Morgan, Sheriff Abe, Deputy Rick Martin, and Cricket. I had to push past Sarah Jenkins, Annie Mae Gregory, and Carrie Smalls just to get next to Mama, who still held Morgan. Snatching the baby from Mama's arms, Cricket was glaring at Birdie Smiley as if she knew it wasn't Mama who meant her baby harm. "You've got a serious problem, crazy woman!" Cricket yelled.

Birdie's slightly-crossed eyes had a pitiful look in them.

Cricket tapped her forehead. "You stole my baby from my car in broad daylight!"

Mama's eyes widened. "You didn't ask Birdie to keep your baby?" she asked Cricket.

Cricket's nostrils flared; she held her baby close to her breast. "She stole Morgan from my car when I went into the Shell station to pay for gas! Thank goodness the lady in the store recognized Birdie's station wagon. And thank goodness Miss Blanche drove up and told us that she'd just seen Birdie walk into this store with Morgan in her arms!"

Sheriff Abe motioned to his deputy to disperse the gathering crowd. "Okay, folks," Rick Martin said, his voice rising above the loudspeaker music, an old Beatles song. "Things are under control now. So go about your business, go on with your shopping."

"*Nobody* is going to leave this store until Cricket and Birdie go!" Carrie Smalls declared loudly.

"If you touch my baby again, I'll kill you, you

hear me," Cricket shrilled, and in her arms little Morgan whimpered.

Birdie bit her bottom lip. Her eyes blinked uncontrollably. But she didn't say a word. Mama studied Birdie's face.

Sheriff Abe, who had known Birdie all her life, spoke. "You come on with me and Rick now," he told Birdie. "We'll get this thing settled properly."

"I'll kill you stiff dead," Cricket said, clutching Morgan so hard the baby started to cry again.

Mama's eyebrows shot up. "Take it easy," she said to Cricket.

"I'll *kill* her if she lays a hand on my baby!"

"No harm has come to Morgan," Mama pointed out. But she looked worried.

"If she so much as looks at my Morgan again, I'll *kill* her. I swear!"

Sheriff Abe eased between Cricket and Birdie.

"Now that you've got that beautiful child back, why don't you take her home?" Mama suggested gently.

Cricket looked down at Morgan and her face lit up. "Don't you *ever* put your hands on my baby again," she warned Birdie Smiley. "If you touch my Morgan again, your behind is mine and nobody is going to keep me from it!"

We watched Cricket sashay away, swearing loud enough for everybody inside and outside of the store to hear her. Abe and Rick waited until she was driving out of the parking lot before they led Birdie toward their patrol car.

"Cricket isn't the most modest girl," Mama

said to me, her eyes following Abe and Rick. "Actually, the girl is a bit on the wild side. I've spent more than a few hours trying to get her to tone down, think about her reputation in this town. I can't say she's paid much attention to what I've told her, though. Still, I know that she loves her baby. I'm convinced that she'd die for Morgan, if it ever came to that. No, it doesn't surprise me, the way Cricket acted. But, Birdie—It just ain't her nature to do something like stealing a baby from an automobile."

"Maybe Birdie's crazy," I said, looking down at my Famous Amos cookies and wondering how many calories were in the whole package. "She certainly acted like she was unbalanced."

Mama shook her head sadly. "I admit there must be something seriously wrong with Birdie. There's no other reason I can think of for her to steal that baby in broad daylight and then bring her inside this store where a crowd of people would see them."

I shrugged. My mind wandered on to Cliff and the way he smiles like Richard Roundtree; the man drives me crazy. "We need to get home. I'm expecting Cliff to call."

Mama nodded as if she knew that my interest in the events that had just taken place had already waned.

I looked down into our shopping cart. We still hadn't picked up the pork roast or the chickens. "Let's get this over with," I told Mama, thinking of the wonderful meals she had promised me.